GREAT CHINA 2

Poetry from classical China

volume two

Translated by
Stean Anthony

Yamaguchi Shoten, Kyoto

山口書店, 京都

Line on the cover from:
「澄邁駅通潮閣」蘇軾・蘇東坡・
Sū Shi (poem 94 below)

余生欲老海南村
帝遣巫陽招我魂
杳杳天低鶻没処
青山一髪是中原

**That mountain range
A line painted
With the finest brush:
BELOVED CHINA!**

Hear my voice at:
http://www35.tok2.com/home/stean2/

Great China 2
© 2012 Stean Anthony
Author's profits,
See end of book for details.
PRINTED IN JAPAN

FOR ALL WHO LOVE
ANCIENT CHINA

Great China 2

Contents: poem number, title, author

Preface		page 10
1.	Sorrow at Parting	Qū Yuán
2.	Storm-winds	Liú Bāng
3.	Song of the Battle of Gāixià	Xiàng Yǔ
4.	Lament for Lǐ Fūrén (Lady Lǐ)	Hàn Wǔdì
5.	Autumn Song	Hàn Wǔdì
6.	Longing for Home	Wūsūn Gōnzhǔ
7.	Water the Horse	Chén Lín
8.	In Praise of Wine	Cáo Cāo
9.	Courage!	Cáo Pī
10.	At Black Tortoise Pond	Cáo Pī
11.	A Sparrow and a Hawk	Cáo Zhí
12.	Poem in Seven Paces	Cáo Zhí
13.	Tumble-weed Rolling	Cáo Zhí
14.	Poet Five Willows	Táo Qián
15.	Going Home 1	Táo Qián
16.	Going Home 2	Táo Qián
17.	Going Home 3	Táo Qián
18.	Going Home 4	Táo Qián
19.	Child Care	Táo Qián
20.	Chrysanthemum Wine	Táo Qián
21.	Life has No Root	Táo Qián
22.	Hunger	Táo Qián

23.	After I've Gone	Táo Qián
24.	Verse Written at Shíbìjīngshè	Xiè Língyùn
25.	At a Quiet Place	Xiè Língyùn
26.	Thinking about You	Xiè Tiào
27.	Xiǎoxiǎo Song	Sū Xiǎoxiǎo
28.	Jade-tree Palace Garden	Chén Shūbǎo
29.	Téngwáng Tower	Wáng Bó
30.	Farewell Xuē Huá	Wáng Bó
31.	Mángshān	Shěn Quánqī
32.	Climbing Guànquè Tower	Wáng Zhīhuàn
33.	Bright for You!	Mèng Hàorán
34.	Verse for a Friend in Changan	Mèng Hàorán
35.	Farewell to Xīn Jiàn	Wáng Chānglíng
36.	At Liángzhōu, Thanking God	Wáng Wéi
37.	Song for the Young	Wáng Wéi
38.	Double Ninth	Wáng Wéi
39.	House on the Wei River	Wáng Wéi
40.	Within Walls	Wáng Wéi
41.	Wénxìng Hut	Wáng Wéi
42.	Jīnzhúlǐng Ridge	Wáng Wéi
43.	The Phoenix Stage	Lǐ Bái
44.	Climbing the Phoenix Tower	Lǐ Bái
45.	Farewell Wāng Lún	Lǐ Bái
46.	Jewel-stair Complaint	Lǐ Bái
47.	Troubled Road	Lǐ Bái

48.	2 Pure Song of Happiness	Lǐ Bái
49.	Song for the Young	Lǐ Bái
50.	Yearning 1	Lǐ Bái
51.	Yearning 2	Lǐ Bái
52.	Lǔdōngmén Boating	Lǐ Bái
53.	Farewell to Dù Fǔ	Lǐ Bái
54.	Remembering Lǐ Bái	Dù Fǔ
55.	Short Verse 2	Dù Fǔ
56.	Beauties by the Water	Dù Fǔ
57.	For Lǐ Bái	Dù Fǔ
58.	Dreaming of Lǐ Bái 1	Dù Fǔ
59.	Old Stronghold Yèchéng	Cén Shēn
60.	Song of the Flute	Cén Shēn
61.	Tower, Yèchéng	Liú Tíngqí
62.	Banished to Lantian	Hán Yù
63.	The Horse Detests Grain	Hán Yù
64.	To Yan Going to Guizhou	Hán Yù
65.	Happy Old Age	Bái Jūyì
66.	Stone City	Liú Yǔxī
67.	Bird Lane	Liú Yǔxī
68.	Jīnshānsì	Zhāng Hù
69.	Before the Tomb of Xiǎoxiǎo	Lǐ Hè
70.	Visiting Kāiyuán Temple	Dù Mù
71.	3 Visiting Shuǐxī Temple	Dù Mù
72.	Below Cháshān	Dù Mù

73.	Cháshān Foregoing the Wine	Dù Mù
74.	Nothing Better Than Peace	Dù Mù
75.	Red Cliffs	Dù Mù
76.	Ford at Wūjiāng	Dù Mù
77.	A Night on Qínhuái	Dù Mù
78.	Sunset	Lǐ Shān Yǐn
79.	Jade Tower Spring	Lǐ Yù
80.	A Nightbird Calls	Lǐ Yù
81.	Field of Red Poppies	Zēng Gǒng
82.	Zhōng Shān	Wáng Ānshí
83.	Early Summer Impressions	Wáng Ānshí
84.	Mooring at Guāzhōu	Wáng Ānshí
85.	Wūjiāng Ford	Wáng Ānshí
86.	For Wáng Ānshí	Sū Shì
87.	For the Abbot of Dōnglín	Sū Shì
88.	Written on the Wall of Xīlín	Sū Shì
89.	Ballad of the Red Cliffs	Sū Shì
90.	Arriving in Huángzhōu	Sū Shì
91.	East Hill	Sū Shì
92.	Not Saying Much Now	Sū Shì
93.	Spring Night	Sū Shì
94.	Looking Towards China	Sū Shì
95.	Garden 1	Lù Yóu
96.	Garden 2	Lù Yóu
97.	Shěn Garden	Lù Yóu

98.	Village Festival	Lù Yóu
99.	Marco Polo Bridge 1	Qián Lóng
100.	Marco Polo Bridge 2	Qián Lóng

Poets' Brief Bios	page 132
A Brief Note on Tones	page 142
Poem Title Index	page 144
First Line Index	page 148
Profile	page 152
Author's Profits	page 153

Preface

This is an anthology of poems from ancient China, dating from c. 300 BCE – 1200 CE. The purpose of the book is to celebrate the achievement of those poets by translating them into a lively modern English idiom. The anthology is also designed to make the poetry of classical China more accessible to a non-Chinese audience.

Although the ancient Chinese language is difficult for a beginner, it is not excessively so, and with the advances in dictionary software, it is possible to read, study and enjoy the poetry in its original form, and also listen to the spoken version, and appreciate the way that the verse sings.

This poetry is a great cultural inheritance of all humanity – it originated in China, but it belongs to us all. For too long it has only been properly appreciated in East Asia: by the Chinese, by Japanese and Koreans, and other well-educated specialists. But year by year China opens her doors wider in friendship. Throughout the world there are more people learning Chinese and coming closer to China, and this book is part of that, and meant to be a bridge for that purpose.

At the same time, English is increasingly the language of

education, and for the first time in the history of the world, the majority of young people in Asia have a reasonably good English ability. This anthology is also for them – between Japan and Korea, China and Taiwan, Vietnam and Thailand, Myanmar and India, Nepal and Afghanistan – English may serve young people as the instrument of friendship and learning. Better English ability is still required, and celebration of Asian culture is good – and so I have made this book.

As in *Manyōshū 365*, translated by Stean Anthony, you will find a comment on each poem. The purpose is to give some background information and also to compensate for liberties taken in the translation. It is impossible to translate directly without writing meaningless lines, and in general I have tried to capture the spirit, even at the cost of being accurate. Some of the comments are also meant to add a poetic lustre to the poem. I also include Chinese characters, because I have always found in translations that I needed to know the original title with an English transcription. Also, the Chinese characters themselves are part of the poetic message, and always were, though originally written by brush, and have been changed and simplified over the years. These characters should not be as foreign to the non-Chinese as they have been – and that is my point.

For a translator and adapter I have to make the extraordinary claim of knowing almost no Chinese. This is a slight exaggeration, since I have been learning Chinese characters for twenty-five years, but I have done so in Japan. I have relied on Japanese editions (which are very good) and on dictionaries. In fact, in myself, by going through the Japanese editions back to the original Chinese poems I am reliving the experience of the early translators, Ernest Fenollosa and Ezra Pound.

Pound's anthology *Cathay* (1915) was for a long time the best translation in English of 李白 Lǐ Bái, whom he called Rihaku, which is his name in Japanese. But nowadays the tools of understanding are close at hand, and I have been able to listen to and enjoy accomplished Chinese readings of each poem, and my study of the poems has taught me Chinese.

In order to appreciate these poems there is much that we need to know, and much of that is beyond my scope in this book. The truth is that it is always better to read poetry in the original, with sensitivity to its own cultural context and according to the rules of its creation. May this book be a bridge to that.

I have included brief biographies of each poet at the end of the book. The commentaries supply some information of that kind, but I have limited myself in this area. A lot of such information is easily accessible on the internet these days, and that information is better quality year by year.

For the books I have used, see the list at the end of this preface. The excellent DVD series produced by NHK, *Kanshi Kikō*, "Journey to Chinese Poetry," and the second one, *Shinkanshi Kikō*, "New Journey to Chinese Poetry," offer beautiful readings of classical Chinese poems in both Chinese and Japanese, with commentary and superb camera-work. This has been very useful, and most of the poems I chose to translate are there.

Acknowledgement
Thank you very much to He Yanran for kindly finding many errors before publication. Thank you also to Chen Wenhui for her helpful comments. Thank you to the website authors and providers.

14

Select Chinese Online Dictionaries and Websites Consulted

MDBG online Chinese-English dictionary:
   http://www.mdbg.net/chindict/chindict.php
Chinese text online project (ancient literature):
   http://ctext.org/
Kanji Dictionaries at:
   http://www.zdic.net/
   http://dict.revised.moe.edu.tw/index.html
Japanese website for Kanshi: 「詩詞世界」
   http://www5a.biglobe.ne.jp/~shici/index.htm

Japanese Editions of Classical Chinese Poetry Consulted

Chūgoku Shijin Senshū Series. (31 vols.) Tokyo: Iwanami Shoten, 1957-, rpt. 「中国詩人選集」

Dù Fǔ. *Toho Shisen*. Ed. Yōichi Kurokawa. Tokyo: Iwanami Shoten, 1994. 「杜甫詩選」

Iritani, Sensuke, trans. *Koshi Sen*. [Ancient Chinese Poems] Tokyo: Asahi Shinbunsha, 1966. 入谷仙介。「古詩選」

Ishikawa, Tadahisa. *NHK Kanshi Kikō*. [Journey to Classic Chinese Poetry] 5 vols. Tokyo: NHK, 1991-1996. 石川忠久監修。「NHK漢詩紀行」

Ishikawa, Tadahisa. *Haku Raku Ten* [Bái Jūyì] *100 sen*. Tokyo: NHK, 2001. 石川忠久。「白楽天100選」

Ishikawa, Tadahisa. *So Tōba [Sū Shì] 100 sen*. Tokyo: NHK, 2001. 石川忠久。「蘇東坡100選」

Ishikawa, Tadahisa. *Kanshi Kikō 100 sen*. [Journey to Classic Chinese Poetry] NHK DVD. 10 vols. Tokyo: NHK, 2004. 石川忠久監修。「漢詩紀行100選」

Ishikawa, Tadahisa. *Shin Kanshi Kikō*. [New Journey to Classic Chinese Poetry] NHK DVD. 10 vols. 制作: AQ Partners, 2009. 石川忠久監修。「新漢詩紀行」

Ishikawa, Tadahisa. *Shin Kanshi Kikō Gaido*. [Guide to New Journey to Classic Chinese Poetry] 6 vols. Tokyo: NHK, 2010. 石川忠久監修。「新漢詩紀行ガイド」

Kanshi Taikei Series (24 vols). Tokyo: Shueisha, 1964-, rpt. 「漢詩大系」

Lĭ Bái. *Ri Haku. Chugoku Shijin Senshu 7 & 8*. Ed. Toshio Takebe. Tokyo: Iwanami Shoten, 1957. 「李白」

Lù Yóu, *Riku Yū Shisen*. Ed. Tomoyoshi Ikkai. Tokyo: Iwanami Shoten, 2007. 「陸游詩選」

Sū Dōngpō, *So Tōba Shisen*. Eds. Tamaki Ogawa & Kazuyoshi Yamamoto. Tokyo: Iwanami Shoten, 1975. 「蘇東坡詩選」

Táo Qián, *Tōenmei Zenshū*. 2 vols. Eds. Shigeo Matsueda & Takeshi Wada. Tokyo: Iwanami Shoten, 1990. 「陶淵明全集」

Tōshi Sanbyaku Shu (3 vols.) [300 poems from the Tang] ed. Makoto Mekada. Tokyo: Heibonsha, 1973-75. 目加田誠。

「唐詩300首」

Uno, Naoto. *Kanshi wo Yomu.* [Tang Poems. NHK Radio Series] 2 vols. Tokyo: NHK, 2009.「漢詩を読む・唐代前後期」

Wáng Wéi. *Ō I: Chugoku Shijin Senshu 6.* Ed. Haruo Tsuru. Tokyo: Iwanami Shoten, 1958.「王維」

English Translations Consulted

Barnstone, Tony and Chou Ping, trans. *The Anchor Book of Chinese Poetry: From Ancient to Contemporary, the Full 3000-year Tradition.* New York: Anchor Books, 1975.

Chang, Edward C. trans. *How to Read a Chinese Poem: A Bilingual Anthology of Tang Poetry.* North Charleston: BookSurge, 2007.

Cooper, Arthur, trans. *Li Po and Tu Fu.* London: Penguin, 1973.

Graham, A. C. trans. *Poems of the Late T'ang.* New York: New York Review Books, 1977.

Hinton, David, trans. *The Selected Poems of T'ao Ch'ien.* Port Townsend, WA: Copper Canyon Press, 1993.

Hinton, David, trans. *The Selected Poems of Li Po.* New York: New Directions, 1996.

Hinton, David, trans. *The Selected Poems of Wang Wei.* New York: New Directions, 2006.

Larsen, Jeanne, trans. *Brocade River Poems: Selected Works of the Tang Dynasty Courtesan Xue Tao.* Princeton: Princeton University Press, 1987.

Minford, John and Joseph S. M. Lau, eds. *An Anthology of Translations: Classical Chinese Literature: Vol. 1, From Antiquity to the Tang Dynasty.* New York: Columbia University Press, 2000.

Pine, Red, trans. *Poems of the Masters: China's Classic Anthology of T'ang and Sung Dynasty Verse.* Port Townsend, WA: Copper Canyon Press, 2003.

Rexroth, Kenneth, trans. *One Hundred More Poems from the Chinese: Love and the Turning Year.* New York: New Directions, 1970.

Rexroth, Kenneth and Ling Chung, trans. *Women Poets of China.* New York: New Directions, 1972.

Watson, Burton, trans. *Selected Poems of Su Tung-p'o.* Port Townsend, WA: Copper Canyon Press, 1994.

Watson, Burton, trans. *The Selected Poems of Du Fu.* New York: Columbia Press, 2002.

Weinberger, Eliot, ed. *The New Directions Anthology of Classical Chinese Poetry.* New York: New Directions, 2003.

Young, David, trans. *Five T'ang Poets: Wang Wei, Li Po, Tu Fu, Li Ho, Li Shang-Yin.* Oberlin OH: Oberlin College Press, 1990.

One   Qū Yuán   屈原

Lísāo   離騷   Sorrow at Parting

Illustrious in birth, a line from heaven,
First poet to the future, Great China!
Born of the tiger, under a tiger moon,
Named for good fortune and auspicious good.
Orchis of the sacral earth,
Flowering spirit I bind about me.
Time's chariot wheels run forward,
To me the strength of the mountain flowers,
And the green weed in the ponds!
Time will not slow spring into autumn,
The autumn grasses wither and fall,
Shall beauty herself be lost?
Thou! Shall you not cast out the impure?
Walk the long path up the mountain.
Great one, give the leads to me,
I'll drive Time's chariot in the van!

Comment
The first 12 lines adapted freely. Qū Yuán is called China's first poet. The content relates to his role as counselor to the sovereign. The poem shifts later into a dream-world of spirit.

Two   Liú Bāng   劉邦

Dàfēnggē   大風歌   Storm-winds

Storm-winds in tumult,
Land in uproar!
Victory, my glory through China,
Now to my home –
I must find a hero or a saint
And make peace for all.

Comment
Written at the end of his life and sung in a banquet when he returned to his home village. The conflict between 劉邦 Liú Bāng and 項羽 Xiàng Yǔ in the background. Liú Bāng founded the Han dynasty, becoming Emperor 漢高祖 Hàn Gāozǔ. 猛士 měngshì, brave warrior, adapted to "hero or saint."

Three   Xiàng Yǔ   項羽

Gāixiàgē   垓下歌   Song of the Battle of Gāixià

All-powerful once,
I could tear up mountains,
My spirit subdued the world!
Time now against me,
Even my beloved steed won't go forward.
If fate is against us what can be done?
But for you, my beloved, for you,
This grief I can't bear.

返歌 · 虞美人 · Yú Měirén's reply

The Han stand around us,
From all sides we hear them sing.
If you great Lord are defeated,
There shall be no life left for me.

Comment
Battle at 垓下歌 in Anhui (202 BC), where the warlord 項羽 Xiàng Yǔ (232-202 BC) (楚 Chǔ), was surrounded and defeated by 劉邦 Liú Bāng (c 250–195 BC) (漢 Han). He held a final banquet, and composed the verse for 虞美人 Yú Měirén, his favourite consort. Famous scene in Peking Opera.

22

Four   Hàn Wǔdì   漢武帝   Liú Chè   劉徹.

Dào Lǐ Fūrén fù   悼李夫人賦
Lament for Lǐ Fūrén (Lady Lǐ)

Silent the silk sleeves,
Dust on the marble floors.
The empty room cold and still.
Fallen leaves at a closed door.
Longing for that lady of beauty
Where shall I find peace?

Comment

Verse attributed to Emperor Hàn Wǔdì, written after the death of his beloved consort Lǐ Fūrén. She was a famed beauty. When she was sick she refused to let the emperor see her face, so that he would always remember her in her prime. Story from 班固 Bān Gù (32-92), *History of the Former Han*, c. 82.

Five   Hàn Wǔdì   漢武帝   Liú Chè   劉徹

Qiū fēng cí   秋風辞   Autumn Song

An autumn breeze and the white clouds fly,
Golden leaves fall, the geese fly home south.
An excellent crown, and pacific fragrant,
The thought of her beauty fills my thought.
Royal barge along the Fénhé river,
Crossing the current, waves ripple downstream.
Flute and drum play! Raise voices in song!
To the heights of joy – and we weep for sorrow.
Youth is gone too soon! Who wants to be old?

Comment
Age 43 (113 BCE), travelling by boat, east on the Yellow River, on the 汾河 Fénhé tributary. He held a banquet on board. In high spirits composed this verse. Crown refers to 茼蒿 Chrysanthemum coronarium. Pacific is Chrysanthemum pacificum, adapted for the names. The original has 蘭 lán, orchid. He is remembering Lǐ Fūrén.

24

Six   Wūsūn Gōngzhǔ   烏孫公主

Bēichóu gē   悲愁歌   Longing for Home

To distant 天 sky I was given for a bride.
I was sent far away to marry Prince Wūsūn.
A dome tent for a house and felt for the walls.
For rice, we had meat, for drink mare's milk.
Thoughts of home never left me, heart sorrowing.
Heaven, make me a swan, I'll fly straight home!

Comment
劉細君 Liú Xìjūn, granddaughter of Emperor Wudi, married to 烏孫昆莫 Wūsūn Kūnmò, prince of the Wūsūn nomads (BCE 105). A political marriage for alliance against the 匈奴 Xiōngnú, a nomad horde threatening the Han. The dome tent is the yurt, in Mongolian, gher. 天 tiān, sky, name for the vast Mongolian plains.

Seven   Chén Lín   陳琳

Yǐn mǎ Chángchéng kū xíng   飲馬長城窟行
Water the Horse

Under the Great Wall
Water the horse from the grotto.
The water so cold
It chills the very bones of the horse.
I went to the officer on the Wall,
"Don't, I beg you, prevent
Those good blokes from Tàiyuán
From being released."
"Things I can and can't do.
Here's the mallet, pound away."
Then I shouted at him,
"Men should fight and die bravely.
Why the hell
Do we have to build this blasted wall!"

Comment
Chén Lín protests about the suffering of the people in his own time (c. 200) by writing about the building of the Great Wall under 秦始皇帝 Emperor Qín Shǐ Huáng Dì (259-210 BCE). "Horse's bones" perhaps a metaphor for China.

Eight   Cáo Cāo   曹操

Duǎngē xíng   短歌行   In Praise of Wine

Life is short bring wine and song,
Life is gone like morning dew.
Days fled by, day after day,
Sorrow like a poison seeps
Unwelcome to the lonely heart.

Hard it is to forget gloom,
Let us throw the darkness out!
Dionysus lend your hand,
Life is short, bring on the wine,
Bring on joy of wine and song!

Comment

The title is more literally "ballad." Said to have been sung before the "Red Cliffs" battle in 208. Dionysus, or Bacchus, is the old classical god of wine and song, a translation here for 杜康 Dù Kāng, the semi-legendary patron of liquor in ancient China. Freely adapted from the first eight lines.

Nine   Cáo Pī   曹丕

Zázhì   雜誌   Courage!

Clouds in the sky north-west
Like parasols in distant procession.
Fate against us, the whirlwind struck,
And we were hurled south-east
Even as far as 紹興市 Shàoxīng.

It's not home,
But I'll be here for a while.
Courage! We'll rise again.
The one from far away
Is always unwelcome.

Comment

A verse about the campaigns in the Three Kingdoms period (c 200-280). This is a period celebrated in classical literature, in particular Luo Guanzhong's *Romance of the Three Kingdoms* (14th century). Cao Pi, unable to unify China, made the famous statement in 225 that "Heaven created the Yangzi to divide the north and south."

28

Ten   Cáo Pī   曹丕

Yú Xuánwǔ pí zuò   於玄武陂作   **At Black Tortoise Pond**

To delight in the world outside the city
Brothers together let us go forth.
The fields stretch to the distance,
Streams and channels run between,
The water purls like young laughter,
Millet and corn promise well.
Water lilies and líng cover the ponds,
Brightly shine the red lotus.
The willows hang down in green curtains,
Inviting us to walk by the water.
Stand on the shoreline, and regard the view.
Hear the geese calling, clanging like bells.
Ripples through floating weed move as the wind passes over.
Forget sorrow, my children! Brighten your heart with me,
Let the time pass with joy in this place.

Comment
菱 líng, water chestnut. The line 流波激悲声 runs against the general sense, so it is translated as "laughter" (line 5). My translation is inaccurate here. My purpose is both poetic and to lighten the tone of this book.

Eleven   Cáo Zhí   曹植

Yětián huángquè xíng   野田黄雀行   A Sparrow and a Hawk

Winds of sorrow stir the tall trees,
In the ocean a deep swell.
Who needs friends
If they've got sharp knives?

Look there at the sparrow by the fence.
Startled by a hawk, it jumped in the net.
The bird-catcher was overjoyed.
A young boy saw the trap and grieved.
He drew his knife, and cut the net.
The sparrow escaped.
The hawk swooped down,
And said thanks.

Comment
Ironic – the third line is more literally, "If they don't have a sharp knife, why would you need them as friends?" The irony is that an act of kindness leads to the opposite result. 黄雀 huángquè, bird to be kept as a pet, perhaps a tree sparrow. The translator supplied the English title.

30

Twelve   Cáo Zhí   曹植

Qībùshī   七步詩   Poem in Seven Paces

Boil the beans and prepare a hot must.
Strain off the ferment and make a soup.
Bean-pods and stalks, burn them under the pan.
Weeping, the beans in the pot sing this song:
We were once of the same root and grew together,
Why are we seethed with such fury now?

Comment

This is a comic verse with a message – Cáo Zhí had fallen out of favour with his brother the Emperor Cáo Pī, and it's a plea for mercy. It was said to have been composed on the command of the emperor in the space of seven paces. 豉 chǐ, fermented beans used for miso.

Thirteen   Cáo Zhí   曹植

Xū jiē piān   吁嗟篇   Tumble-weed Rolling

Tumble-weed rolling
Distant come tumbling
Over and over,
Far from the root-birth
Unresting journey
High up to heaven
Low long the plains,
Distant come rolling,
Will you not turn
To the place that was home?

Wind like destiny
Hastens you on,
All points of compass
Passed through in time,
Resilient survivor,
Lifted again,
High over mountains,
Unresting journey!
Will you not go back
To the place that was home?

Comment

Freely adapted, last lines omitted. Title supplied by translator. Cáo Zhí, oppressed by his brother the Emperor and his successor, laments his life of exile. Last lines: "So my life was spent! | To be woodland grasses, | Burnt up in a moment, | Better by far!" 転蓬 zhuǎngpéng, fleabane, (Asteraceae) tumbleweed.

Fourteen   Táo Qián   陶潛   Táo Yuānmíng   陶淵明

Wǔ liǔ Xiānshēng zhuàn   五柳先生傳   **Poet Five Willows**

Nobody knew where the teacher came from
And his family name was unknown.
There were five willows by his house,
And he took his pen-name from them.

He was a modest man of few words.
A great reader, but not one to force the sense.
When he found a passage he liked,
He was so happy that he even forgot to eat.

By nature he loved good wine, but so poor
That he couldn't drink much.
When the cupboard was empty
Family and friends would leave him a bottle,

Or invite him round, and he would drink deep,
And totter back home happily drunk.
He wasn't one to fret
Over whether he was staying too long.

34

He lived in a ramshackle cottage,
At the mercy of wind and rain.
He wore an old patched-up linen robe.
And if the gourd was empty, he'd say

So what! I delight in the making of a verse,
And discover there the way I feel,
I don't care a whit for the way they think,
I'm keeping with this, and so to the end.

Comment

Omitting the last few lines of this passage. A biographical fragment. The word "happily" is added. 箪瓢 dānpiáo, gourd, a bowl for food or drink. 得失 déshī, the profit and loss, success or failure, translated as "the way they think." Táo rejects conventional values, and his brave individualism is an inspiration.

Fifteen   Táo Qián 陶潛   Táo Yuānmíng 陶淵明

Guī qù lái xī cí   歸去來分辞   Going Home 1

God knows, when I got that job
All I could think was
Yes, I want to leave.
Back now to my true home!
It was my own nature
Forthright, down to earth –
How could I do violence
To myself, twisting my soul
To a shape to please others?
To ruin what I naturally am?
In fact, I'd suffered before,
And had to glue my lips shut,
Hating every single moment.
Shame and misery went on,
Day after day, myself in conflict.
Just one more year, I said,
At harvest time, I'll take wing
Under cover of the dark,
And fly to freedom in the south.

Comment

Adapted from part of the preface to the poem, section beginning 及少日眷然有帰. A heartwarming protest at the petty life of administrative bureaucracy, longing for rural simplicity and goodness (405, age 41). This is the same theme found in his poems in *Great China 1*, "Homecoming 1 & 2" p. 22.

Sixteen   Táo Qián 陶潜   Táo Yuānmíng 陶淵明

Guī qù lái xī cí   歸去来分辞   Going Home 2

On our way, then, homeward bound!
The land is overgrown, home then!
Too long my spirit the slave of my body,
No point in lamentation now,
No use regretting what's gone,
Let me lay hold on the good that's coming.
Sure I went wrong, a wrong turning,
But it's not over yet, the best thing
I did was to leave that bureaucratic hell!

The boat lifts on the waves,
A gentle swell lifts and falls,
The breeze fills my robes.
I ask a fellow passenger about the route,
The morning light pale,
The way ahead still not clear.

Comment
"Going Home" is a free adaptation of parts of this long poem.

38

Seventeen   Táo Qián   陶潛   Táo Yuānmíng   陶淵明

Guī qù lái xī cí   歸去来分辞   Going Home 3

There's my front door at last!
Overjoyed, I run forward,
The amahs come forward with smiles,
The infants wait by the porch,
The garden in disarray,
But the pine and 菊 jú are still there.
The children take my hand and we go inside,
A decanter of best wine full to the brim,
So I pour out a glass straightaway,
Happy as I look upon the garden trees,
My elbows on the south window-sill.
It's small, it's comfortable, and it's home.

Day by day the garden comes into shape,
My gate shut now to the busy world.
With my staff to support me, I'll grow old
Taking a rest now and then,
Lifting my gaze to the view,
Carefree the clouds on the mountains,
Wearied the birds wing homeward,
Evening comes and the sun goes down,

My hand rests on the lonely pine,
And frankly, I don't want to leave.

Comment

菊 jú, chrysanthemum. I use the Chinese because the English word unbalances the line. The flower had positive sacred associations in ancient China, a symbol of goodness and long life.

40

Eighteen   Táo Qián   陶潛   Táo Yuānmíng   陶淵明

Guī qù lái xī cí   歸去来分辞   Going Home 4

Shall I grieve now as I think our life so short,
The spirit a little while to lodge in this clay?
Let me live in the river's flow, a cosmic process,
Unquestioning and accepting.

Why do we always seek what's not there,
Busy with idols and dreams?
I've no wish for position or wealth,
Neither a sage nor a saint I'll be.

The sky clear blue, I'll go forth, my staff to support me,
To the fields, or climb the East Hill,
My flute on the evening breeze.
By the bright waters a lovely verse,
My body will be the season which changes,
No care and no worry. Heaven be the driver!

Comment
寓形宇內復幾時
yù xíng yǔ nèi fù jǐ shí
How long indeed may we live beneath this sky?

Nineteen   Táo Qián 陶潛   Táo Yuānmíng 陶淵明

Zézǐ 責子 Child Care

Head white with old age, face wrinkled with care!
Blessed with five sons but they don't want to study.
舒 Shū, already sixteen, useless fellow, a born idler.
宣 Xuān, nearly fifteen, doesn't like books.
雍 Yōng and 端 Duān both thirteen,
Can't tell the difference between 6 or 7.
通子 Tōngzǐ almost nine,
Pears and chestnuts all his desire.
If this be the fatherhood given to me,
I shall drink what is in my glass!

Comment

Perhaps ironic, to spur his sons to their books. In the original, line 7 志学 zhìxué, "aim to study" there's a reference to Confucius, *Analects* chapter 2.4 吾十有五而志於學 "at fifteen my aim was to study." See Stean Anthony, *Kǒngzǐ 136* (Yamaguchi, Kyoto: 2012) poem 10.

42

Twenty   Táo Qián 陶潛   Táo Yuānmíng 陶淵明

Yǐnjiǔ 飲酒 7 Chrysanthemum Wine

Fragrant chrysanthemum autumn's glory!
I pick the petals wet with dew,
Wine to banish sorrow 忘憂 wàngyōu!
I float them in a glass of sake,
That world I leave behind
To deepen this feeling,
Glass after glass I drink on my own,
The bottle pours and the glass is empty.
The sun sets and quiet comes.
The crows caw as they fly to the wood.
Under the east eaves,
I'm released into freedom –
For a while thus to live this life.

Comment
Number seven in a twenty poem series called 飲酒 "drinking sake." Chrysanthemum a purging flower, drunk with sake at 重陽 Chóngyáng, the Double Ninth festival, (ninth day of ninth lunar month), clearing away all badness. He says that he has achieved the wisdom to be content with his life. Drinking sake leads the poets to spiritual wisdom.

Twenty-One   Táo Qián 陶潛   Táo Yuānmíng 陶淵明

Zá shī 雜詩 1   Life has No Root

Life has no root, leaf falls through air,
Whirlwind spins up the dust on the road,
Borne on the wind scattered everywhere,
Today tomorrow this body won't last.

Born upon earth all are brothers,
Beyond kindred, the world one family!
This chance of happiness should be taken,
Share joy with neighbor and friend.

Youth will not return,
Today won't be here tomorrow,
Lose not the time – to your books!
Time runs on and won't wait.

Comment
First one in a series of twelve verses written on various occasions. "Joy" in line 8 translates 斗酒 dǒu jiǔ, a measure of wine. The poem reads like three separate apothegms. The actual title is literally "miscellaneous verse." Title above supplied by the translator, as often in this book.

Twenty-Two   Táo Qián   陶潛   Táo Yuānmíng   陶淵明

Qǐshí   乞食   Hunger

Hunger drags me from my door,
Impells me not knowing where,
Here I find myself in a village,
I knock on the door but words are frozen.

My journey there was not in vain.
The master knew just how I felt.
He shared his goodness with me,
We talked until the sun went down.

Glass followed glass of good wine
Joy in this new heart companion,
The words we sang we put in bright verse.

Once an old woman saved a boy.
You saved me with your kindness.
Though I've no skill, I'll say thanks here!

Comment

The story referred to comes from 韓信 Hán Xìn, (d. 196 BCE) a general of the first Han emperor, Liú Bāng. When he was young and very poor and starving, there was an old woman washing clothes in a river, and she gave him some rice, and saved his life. This is adapted slightly omitting the last line.

46

Twenty-Three   Táo Qián   陶潛   Táo Yuānmíng   陶淵明

Nǐ wǎngē shī   擬挽歌詩 1   After I've Gone

When there is life, there will be death.
If we die young (or not), it's what we're given.
At yesterday's sunset business as usual,
But today your name's in the big black book.
The soul is freed, where shall she go?
The corpse is stretched on the funeral cart.
The youngest weeps for his Dad,
My dear friend touches my hand and laments.
In life's struggle, did I win, did I lose?
With the sheep or the goats, who can say?

In ten thousand years who will care
About worldly success or failure.
Only one regret remains –
That I wasted the chance I had
To drink more of that excellent wine!

Comment
挽歌 a dirge, first one in a series of three. Imagining his own funeral. 千秋萬歲後 qiān qiū wàn suì hòu, a thousand autumns, ten thousand years from now.

47

Twenty-Four   Xiè Língyùn   謝靈運

Shíbìjīngshè huán hú zhōng zuò   石壁精舍還湖中作
Verse Written at Shíbìjīngshè

Sun-up and sunset, how they differ!
The mountains above the river, pure light
Delighting our senses in the changing day.
I may rest here, and forget time.

I was at the valley-head before sunrise,
In the boat, and the sun now setting.
The wooded slopes deepen in twilight,
The clouds glow red. On the pond surface
The caltrop and lotus shine upon each other,
The reed and the millet together sway.

The wind hastens, I hurry on the southern path.
At home I stretch out by the east door,
Content and unburdened, happy at last.
To the traveller looking for relief,
This is the path you should walk, my friend.

Comment

Xiè is celebrated as the first great Chinese landscape poet. The title of this poem is the name of the hut that he used for study in his village, 始寧 Shǐníng.

Twenty-Five Xiè Língyùn 謝靈運

Guò shǐ níng shù 過始寧墅 At a Quiet Place

Climbing the mountain, valleys and ridges,
Crossing the water, there are no more hills.
The cliffs are steep, behind them summits recede,
Islands in the river, white sandy shores.
Cloud cover sits on the lonely alp,
Green bamboo rustles over bright waves.

Comment
This is an excerpt from the middle section of a 22 line poem, lines 11-16, from 山行窮登頓. A vision of tranquillity.

50

Twenty-Six   Xiè Tiào   謝朓

Yù jiē yuàn   玉階怨   Thinking about you

Evening, and I lower the jade curtains.
Fireflies darting delight the heart.
A long night mending the silk gown,
My thoughts run upon you
And I just can't stop.

Comment
Poem as by a court lady grieving for love. Xiè Tiào (called "Little Xiè" to distinguish him from his relative 謝靈運 Xiè Língyùn, called "Big Xiè"). His elegant verses influenced the Tang poets, especially Li Bai. The title literally "Jade step lamentation" refers to an old melody – a lament for neglect in love, abandoned to the palace step.

51

Twenty-Seven   Sū Xiǎoxiǎo   蘇小小

Sū Xiǎoxiǎo gē   蘇小小歌   Xiǎoxiǎo Song

I'm in the gorgeous rainbow-painted palanquin.
You're on a horse with sky-blue coats.
Where shall we join our hearts in one?
Must it be in that mound,
Under the pine and cypress?

Comment

蘇小小 Sū Xiǎoxiǎo, a legendary courtesan of Hangzhou, reputed to have been one of the two most beautiful women who ever lived. (The other was Yang Guifei.) This is a verse attributed to her, found in the collection 古樂府. Her tomb is situated by Xilin Bridge on West Lake. It was restored in 2004.

52

Twenty-Eight   Chén Shūbǎo   陳叔宝

Yù shù hòu tíng huā   玉樹後庭花   Jade-tree Palace Garden

Graceful roof, flowering meadows, the elegant tower –
Beautiful maidens bright-faced by the walls,
In the doorways, lovely girls like a picture,
Smiling they appear through the screen,
Coquettish, they capture the heart,
Like dew in the blossom a beautiful face.
Like moonlight on a jade-sculpted tree
Light fills the old palace garden.

Comment

The last emperor of the Chen dynasty, incompetent in matters of state, but known for his love of wine and beautiful women, and skill in poetry. He reigned from 582-589. This verse praises the beauty of his favorite consorts, in particular 張麗華 Zhāng Lìhuá.

53

Twenty-Nine   Wáng Bó   王勃

Téngwáng gé 滕王阁 Téngwáng Tower

Téngwáng Tower, gaze upon quiet waters!
Heard no more
The lovely jade clinking,
Dance and music, bright bells.

In the morning look out and see
As on painted walls, clouds fly from Nánpǔ.
Part the pearl screen in the evening,
Rainfall on the mountain.

Unfettered clouds, the water's deep blue
Continue unchanging,
But time goes forward and stars alter,
So many autumns ran by.

Prince in the Tower, where are you now?
Beyond the balustrade,
The great river flows on,
The sad truth of our lives.

54

Comment

Wáng Bó en route south to visit his banished father (675), wrote this about Téngwáng Tower, built by 滕王李元嬰 Prince Téngwáng Lǐ Yuányīng (653) in 南昌 Nánchāng, Jiangxi. One of the great Chinese Towers.

Thirty   Wáng Bó   王勃

Bié Xuē Huá   別薛華   Farewell Xuē Huá

1 Said farewell to you
   Far too many times!
   Hard road upwards.

2 On your own now,
   Sad and sorrowful.
   Which way to go?

3 A long way and lonely,
   That you'll be walking.
   A thousand miles.

4 Not a hundred years
   Can tell the sorrow
   That I feel!

5 You and I together,
   In the heart 心 thought,
   Where is peace found?

6 Should our lives
   For us both
   Be such bitter suffering?

7 Shall we leave?
   Shall we stay?
   Be or not be, do not ask!

8 Just this, by love,
   We shall meet in dreams
   You and I.

Comment

Farewell to a good friend. The directness and poignancy of the poem is reminiscent of early Japanese classical poetry. In the last verse I have added two words "by love."

Thirty-One   Shěn Quánqī   沈佺期

Mángshān   邙山   Mángshān

The tombs of the ancestors stand
Rank upon rank on Mángshān.
A thousand autumns gone by,
Long they've stood above Luoyang.
Evening falls on the city,
Someone sings, a bell sounds.
On the mountains who will hear
The sigh of the pines?

Comment
Mángshān near Luoyang in Henan, where there are many Han, Wei and Jin dynasty royal tombs. 松柏 sōng bǎi, pine and cypress.

Thirty-Two   Wáng Zhīhuàn   王之渙

Dēng Guànquè lóu   登鸛雀樓   Climbing Guànquè Tower

Behind the western mountains the brightness sinks.
黃河 Huáng Hé flows onward to the sea.
That my gaze go further, even a thousand leagues,
I climb the tower to a higher stage.

Comment

The tower is located near Yongjishi, in Shanxi, where the Yellow River flowing south turns abruptly east. The sea cannot be seen from the tower, but climbing up high gives one the feeling of vision. The tower has just been reconstructed (2002). 黃河 Huáng Hé, Yellow River. 鸛鵲 Guànquè, white stork.

Thirty-Three   Mèng Hàorán   孟浩然

Sù jiàn dé jiāng   宿建德江   Bright for You!

On the quiet sand-bar
Moor in the mist.
At sunset a journeyer,

Sadness returns.
Wide the green fields,
Sky sleeps on the trees.

In the river
Water runs pure,
Bright moon,
Bright for you!

Comment

天低树 tiān dī shù, sky (or the heavens) rests on the trees, referring to the mist or cloud. 建德 Jiàndé, this is a river, located in Zhejiang, Hangzhou. The bright moonlight is felt to be a gift. Title is supplied by the translator.

Thirty-Four   Mèng Hàorán   孟浩然

Sòng yǒu rù jīng   送友入京   Verse for a friend in Changan

Risen on a cloud, you to the heights,
And I to the mountains homeward.
Clouds and mountains, the path divides.
My tears soak my dark-brown robes.

Comment
A verse for a friend (Wáng Wéi) who passed the examination, which he failed to do, and heads homeward. 薜蘿衣 bì luó yī, robe worn to conceal one's identity.

Thirty-Five   Wáng Chānglíng   王昌齡

Fú róng lóu sòng Xīn Jiàn   芙蓉楼送辛漸
Farewell to Xīn Jiàn

Cold rain on the river nightfall 長江 Chángjiāng south,
Farewell at dawn, lonely appears 楚山 Chǔshān.
If you were to meet my friend in 洛陽 Luòyáng
Say that my heart is ice in a white jade jar.

Comment

Fúrónglóu, an old tower in Zhènjiāng, Jiāngsū where he says farewell to his friend Xīn Jiàn. "The heart is bright and clear like ice" is what it really means. A common epithet. He is not unfeeling. The point is the sadness he hides. 長江 Chángjiāng, Yangtze. 楚山 Chǔshān, hill on the opposite bank.

Thirty-Six   Wáng Wéi   王維

Liángzhōu sàishén   涼洲賽神
At Liángzhōu, Thanking God

Few leave the fort at Liángzhōu.
Over there in the hills,
A hundred leagues maybe,
Dust-storms
In the hooves of the Khan.
I can hear the drum and pipes
Of our soldiers below.
For the god of the riders
There's a feast-day east of the fort,
Perhaps we should pray too.

Comment

虜 lǔ, these are the barbarian peoples at the borders of Tang China, see poem 36 in *Great China 1*, Lǐ Bái, "Midnight Song". The Khan is used generically to refer to the Turkic and Mongolian peoples, who divided the continent with China.

Thirty-Seven   Wáng Wéi   王維

Shào nián xíng   少年行   Song for the Young

Xīnfēng champagne a thousand bucks.
Bright young Xiányáng crowd, in high spirits,
Salut! Here's to you met so happily today.
Porsches under willows by the blue tower.

Comment

First poem in a series of four. 新豊 Xīnfēng, east of 長安 Chángān, famous for rice wine. 咸陽 Xiányáng, old capital, here used for Chángān (which is now called 西安 Xīān). 高樓 high tower, translated as blue tower, where the escort girls serve drinks. Horses (translated as porsche sports-cars) tied to the willows.

Thirty-Eight   Wáng Wéi   王維

Jiǔyuè jiǔrì yì shāndōng xiōngdì   九月九日憶山東兄弟
Double Ninth, Missing My Brothers

Alone in a foreign land, a foreigner myself.
Autumn again and home in the thoughts.
Climbing a hill far away, my brothers
Daub the red berries on for luck –
One who is absent wishes he were there!

Comment

Age 17, missing his family. Wang, highly gifted, passed the exams age 15 and went to Chángān. 重陽 Chóng Yáng, Double Ninth festival (ancient Tao festival, ninth day of ninth month). This involved smearing red berry paste on the face to ward off misfortune and climbing a hill. 茱萸 zhūyú, Cornus officinalis (dogwood with attractive red fruit).

64

Thirty-Nine   Wáng Wéi   王維

Wèi chuān tián jiā   渭川田家   House on the Wei River

Evening sun falls across the old village,
Along the path the cattle walk home,
The old man thinks about the herdboy,
Leaning on his stick,
Standing in his humble doorway.
A pheasant whirs, the wind sings through the barley,
The silkworm sleeps, the mulberry has gone.
The laborer picks up the hoe, and sets off,
Stops, and shares a few friendly words.
I'm seized by longing for this peace,
And sing a verse from an old song:
Our strength decays, let us now return!
If it weren't for you, O prince,
Why should I be thus soaked by the dew?

Comment

Late autumn. A Chinese pastoral idyll, like a picture. The leaves of the mulberry have fallen, the silkworm season is over. Last three lines are expanded and quoted from *The Book of Songs*, Lessons from the States, 邶風 Bèifēng, Odes of Bèi, 式微 Shìwèi.

65

Forty Wáng Wéi 王維

Sòng Mèng liù guī xiāng yáng 送孟六帰襄陽
Within Walls

Close the gate and stay within walls,
Shut out the world and its trouble,
This is best,
So I send you on your way home.

Drink good wine, sing a happy song.
Laugh when you read a book, an old friend!
Spend your life like this –
Inspiration unbroken, write your best work!

Comment
Wáng says goodbye to 孟浩然 Mèng Hàorán. The last line is more lit. "without trouble, write and dedicate 子虛 Zǐ Xū" – a work written by 司馬相如 Sīmǎ Xiāngrú (179-117 BCE) Han poet. It gained him a job as a court poet. "Within walls" is not a hermit-life, but in retirement from public duties.

Forty-One   Wáng Wéi   王維

Wén xìng guǎn   文杏館   Wénxing Hut

Beam of apricot wood for the house.
Fragrant incense roof across.
Unexpected clouds behind the building –
Rain upon our world in departing.

Comment

Third verse in the 輞川 Wǎngchuān (Wheel-rim River) sequence of poems. 香茅 xiāngmáo, lemongrass used in the reed thatching, translated as "fragrant incense" – retreat from the world, prayer and meditation. 人間 rén jiān, the world of humanity, as opposed to the divine.

67

Forty-Two   Wáng Wéi   王維

Jīnzhúlǐng   斤竹嶺   Jīnzhúlǐng Ridge

Tall the lovely bamboo shade the path,
Green water ripples through the leaves,
Walk the cool dark of 商山 Shāngshān,
Not even the woodsman knows this way.

Comment
Fourth verse in the 輞川 Wǎngchuān (Wheel-rim River) sequence of poems. Title refers to a mountain near the hut. In communion with nature, going further than even the woodsman can know.

Forty-Three   Lǐ Bái   李白

Dēng Jīnlíng fènghuáng tái   登金陵鳳凰台
The Phoenix Stage

On the dancing-stage the Phoenix danced,
Now she has gone, the river runs sadly.
In the 吳 Wú palace garden
Wild flowers have hidden the paths,
The old courtiers of 晉 Jìn
Sleep now under earth.

Distant through the wide reach
Of heaven the mountains appear.
A single stream divides into two
Watering 白鷺洲 Báilù fields.
Thick clouds hide the sun.
Changan faraway, sorrow comes again!

Comment

金陵 Jīnlíng is 南京 Nánjīng. Visiting a ruined temple on a hill, remembering the Three Kingdoms (c. 220-280). 白鷺洲 Báilù, a park in Nanjing. The Chinese Phoenix is an embodiment of Buddhist law, signifying enlightenment; in the west, reborn from flame, a symbol of resurrection.

Forty-Four   Lǐ Bái   李白

Dēng Jīnlíng fènghuáng tái   登金陵鳳凰台
Climbing the Phoenix Tower

Here on this tower
Long ago the Phoenix danced
She has gone! And there, as ever,
You go, great river, down to the sea.
Flowers hide the paths in the palace gardens.
The courtiers of Jin are there under earth.
Distant hills half-hidden float in the sky.
Here the sandbank divides the flow.
How the clouds hide the sun!
長安! 長安!
Joy not in my mind,
Thy humble servant
In sorrow!

Comment

Another translation of the same poem. 長安 Chángān, old name for 西安 Xīān, the capital. For Lǐ Bái it meant joy and civilization. 安 ān, various meanings: contentment, calm, stillness, safety, peace.

Forty-Five   Lǐ Bái   李白

Zèng Wāng Lún   贈汪倫   Farewell Wāng Lún

All aboard – cast off, I said,
But from the quay a crowd started singing.

Peach blossom above, deep water below.

But those good waters are not as deep
As your love for me
Wāng Lún!

Comment

Age 55, composed on the occasion of saying good bye to Wāng Lún, with whom he had been drinking sake. The poem refers to the reservoir 桃花潭 Táohuātán (literally peach blossom pond) located in Anhui. Wāng Lún and the villagers are on the quay dancing and singing farewell.

Forty-Six   Lǐ Bái   李白

Yù jiē yuàn   玉階怨   Jewel-stair Complaint

The jewel-jade steps shine with dew.
A long night waiting,
Even my silken slippers are wet.

Jingling like glass-bells,
I lower the crystal curtain
And gaze on the bright autumn moon.

Comment
Waiting in the palace for the beloved. 羅襪 luó wà, silk stockings – translated as slippers. The last line musical: 玲瓏望秋月 línglóng wàng qīu yuè, línglóng is the clink of jewels (onomatopoeia), or exquisite or bright, referring to the moon. Compare poem 26 above by Xiè Tiào.

Forty-Seven   Lǐ Bái   李白

Xíng lù nán   行路難   Troubled Road

Oak-barrelled tawny, one thousand guineas,
On the green jade, the oyster ten thousand –
But I lower my glass, drop the chopsticks,
Whip out my sword, and glare round distracted.

Should I descend the Yellow River, it's frozen.
Should I wish to climb the mountain,
The sky's dark with snow.
Quietly I sit in the valley fishing,
Longing all the while to be on a boat
Sailing west to the sun.

My life a troubled road!
An unsteady airstream,
Multiple junctions before me,
Where shall I find peace?
A warm wind will come to smooth these waves,
I'll lift sail then and cross the sea.

Comment
Age 44, forced to leave Changan, he went to Luoyang, where he met Du Fu. Here he expresses the difficulties he suffered. Sailing to the sun means winning recognition at court.

行路難 行路難
多岐路 今安在!

Xíng lù nán, xíng lù nán,
Duō qí lù, jīn ān zài!

74

Forty-Eight   Lǐ Bái   李白

Qīng píng diào cí   清平調詞   2 Pure Song of Happiness

Loveliest peony, the dew fragrant.
Her beauty lost in the cloud – bitter sorrow!
Shall we ask the palace who is like her?
Bright-winged swallow, you without compare!

Comment

Second poem offered to 楊貴妃 Yáng Guìfēi (719-756) on order of the emperor. Second line refers to a beautiful mountain goddess who turned to cloud and rain, morning and evening on 巫山 Wūshān, Mount Wu. There was a beauty in the old palace called 飛燕 Fēiyàn, lit. flying swallow (See also *Great China 1* p. 66).

Forty-Nine   Lǐ Bái   李白

Shào nián xíng   少年行   Song for the Young

Young tuxedos to the 金市 Jīnshì bars.
Spring breeze behind you,
Silver stirrups, white steeds,
Fallen blossom under feet.

Where shall we do the town?
Serving drinks, over there,
Girls from Samarkand –
And laughing there they go.

Comment
五陵年少 wǔlíng niánshào, the young and wealthy. 金市 Jīnshì, a town to the west of Changan. 胡姬 hújī, young women slaving in the pleasure quarters, originally from the far west, i.e. foreign women. Compare poem 37 by Wang Wei. Also poem 96 by Du Mu in *Great China 1*.

76

Fifty   Lǐ Bái   李白

Cháng xiāng sī   長相思   Yearning 1

Longing for you, I'm in Changan.
Autumn now,
The crickets sing by the golden well.
A light frost fallen, it's cold.
The bamboo mat's like ice.
My sole lamp doesn't give enough light.
Shall I put from me this yearning?
Pulling up the blind to gaze on the moon,
Sighing in vain for so long,
O lady your beauty in flower,
Up there beyond the clouds,
Deep azure of holy heaven.

Comment

First eight lines of this poem. Last lines omitted so that this version has an upbeat nuance, for the tone of this book to be lighter. The original ends with 長相思 摧心肝 cuī xīn gān, unending longing, enough to break the heart.

Fifty-One   Lǐ Bái   李白

Cháng xiāng sī   長相思   Yearning 2

Waiting for the day's end,
The flowers now in mist.
Moonlight like fine silk,
Yet sorrowing so I can't sleep.
When I play the old zither
My hands on the phoenix
Depicted on the bridge,
And taking the 蜀 Shǔ harp
I pluck the mandarin strings, married bliss!
There's sense in these song lines,
But who'll understand me?
My love on a spring breeze goes to you
At 燕然 Yànrán, blue heaven's between us.

Comment
燕然 Yànrán, mountain, west China. Two musical instruments here. 趙瑟 old chinese harp from 趙 zhào, an ancient kingdom, and 蜀琴 a harp from 蜀 old kingdom (Sichuan). Last four lines cut.

78

Fifty-Two   Lǐ Bái   李白

Lǔ dōng mén fàn zhōu èr shǒu   魯東門汎舟二首
Lǔdōngmén Boating

The heavens in the water mirrored
As the setting sun strikes the sand.
If rapids run, the pebbles roll,
And the water eddies and circles.
Light my boat beneath the moon,
Floating through narrow straits,
Yet to our regret we find
The lovely snow on the mountains gone!

Comment
Boating on the river in 兗州 Yǎnzhōu, 山東 Shāndōng, written when the author was about 40 years old. Originally two verses with this title. I have translated one (as in my source).

Fifty-Three   Lǐ Bái   李白

Lǔ jùn dōng Shímén sòng Dù èr fǔ   魯郡東石門送杜二甫
Farewell to Dù Fǔ

How many days have passed
Since we saluted one another
With wine and said farewell?
I've walked up the hills
And gazed on the waters
From high platforms.
Well, we said goodbye,
But on the road to 石門 Shímén
Let's unstop the good wine.
The autumn wind ruffles the 泗水 Sishuǐ river –
The water's fallen,
Bright the reflection of 徂徠 Cúlái.
We are like tumbleweed, tumbling far – while we can,
Let's drink another glass together again!

Comment
745, farewell to Dù Fǔ, NE of 曲阜 Qūfù, 山東 Shāndōng. A year spent together, they drank many glasses, but never to meet again. 徂徠 Cúlái, mountain, also means arrive and depart – suggesting the threshold of the next world.

Fifty-Four   Dù Fǔ   杜甫

Chūn rì yì Lǐ Bái   春日憶李白
Remembering Li Bai on a Spring Day

Lǐ Bái, who can compare with you?
High above us in another sphere,
Your verse is bright like 庾信 Yǔ Xìn,
Brilliant like 鮑照 Bào Zhào.

Spring in the trees north of 渭 Wèi,
I'm thinking about you,
Now east of 長江 Chángjiāng,
You'll be viewing the sunset on the clouds.

Together may we once again, I pray,
Share a glass of good wine
And engage the mind
With the beauty of Great Chinese verse!

Comment
Replying to Lǐ Bái's verse 魯郡東石門送杜二甫 Farewell to Dù Fǔ (poem 53 above). 庾信 Yǔ Xin, poet (513-581). 鮑照 Bào Zhào, poet (414?-466). 渭 Wèi, Wei river.

Fifty-Five   Dù Fǔ   杜甫

Juéjù   絕句   Short Verse 2

River through hills
Sun long in evening
Spring breeze through flowers
Beauty now and fragrance.
Swallows gather mud for their nests,
On a warm sandbank
I sleep, 鴛鴦 yuānyāng.

Comment
764, age about 53. The title refers to the five-character four-line structure of the verse. 鴛鴦 yuānyāng, mandarin ducks, lit. the drake and hen, signifying a loving marriage. Burton Watson has "where sands are warm, mandarin ducks doze."

82

Fifty-Six   Dù Fǔ   杜甫

Lì rén xíng   麗人行   Beauties by the Water

上巳 Shàngsì performed to make all good,
Blue skies above,
The court beauties gather by the water.
How graceful they are, how elegant,
How full of life! Perfect skin,
Perfect shape, perfect hair!
The gorgeous satin they wear
Reflects the spring flowers,
Gold thread makes a peacock,
Silver thread a 麒麟 qílín,
On their sidelocks a kingfisher feather,
And the edge of their robe
Weighed down by a thousand pearls!

Comment

Age 42. First ten lines of a long poem about the court. 上巳 Shàngsì, a Tao purification ritual carried out beside running water on March 3 (lunar calendar). 麒麟 qílín, kylin, Chinese unicorn.

Fifty-Seven   Dù Fǔ   杜甫

Zèng Lǐ Bái   贈李白   For Lǐ Bái

Autumn again, reliving the time –
Like old tumble weeds rolling,
We didn't find that brilliant earth,
葛洪 Gě Hóng forgive us!
Day after day mad songs and sake,
Free spirits abandoned to joy –
And who was the reason!

Comment
Sent to Lǐ Bái. 葛洪 Gě Hóng (284-363), Tao philosopher, admired by Lǐ Bái. The place in which they had stayed was known as a source for 丹砂 dānshā, cinnabar, a red mineral earth, used in Chinese alchemy. For the younger and more staid Dù Fǔ, Lǐ Bái was a mad liberating Tao spirit.

84

Fifty-Eight   Dù Fǔ   杜甫

Mèng Lǐ Bái   夢李白   Dreaming of Lǐ Bái 1

Death dividing friends is sorrow
But parted by life may be greater.
Poisonous mists, in exile on the lower river.
No letter comes from you though I yearn –
Beloved friend, you appear in my dream,
Bright as daylight I know
It's because

Comment
759. With the outbreak of rebellion and chaos in China, news came that Lǐ Bái had been arrested and sent into exile. Dù Fǔ wrote this verse. They had spent 744-5 together but they were not to meet again. First six lines of this poem.

Fifty-Nine   Cén Shēn   岑參

Dēng gǔ Yèchéng   登古鄴城   Old Stronghold Yèchéng

Dismounting and entering Yèchéng
Nothing remains but sad dereliction.
Breeze from the east fans the field-fires,
The sun sets on the Cloud-lifted Halls.
In the south corner where the tower stands,
The streams flow east and do not return.
From the old emperor's palace
The courtiers have gone,
Year by year
For whom then does the lovely spring bloom?

Comment
武帝 Wǔdì, translated as old emperor, here refers to 曹操 Cáo Cāo. The ruins of Yèchéng are located in 河北省臨漳 Héběishěng Línzhāng. 飛雲殿 Fēiyúndiàn, literally flying cloud palace, translated as cloud-lifted halls. Cáo Cāo's grave mound was viewed from the tower.

Sixty   Cén Shēn   岑参

Hújiā gē   胡笳歌   Song of the Flute

The sad fife's sweet song,
The boys leave for the frontier.
Lingers the song,
Enchanting the sense,
Before it ends they have gone.

Comment

A short verse adapted from 12 lines. 胡笳 hújiā, a flute played by tribes in the north-west. There was conflict at the western frontier, and troops were sent west on garrison duty. Poems on this theme were common in the Tang period.

Sixty-One   Liú Tíngqí   劉庭琦

Tóngquètái   銅雀台   Tower, Yèchéng

Bright towers and silver halls are dust!
By the running water, Cáo Cāo,
Your spirit sleeps under earth –
As I look west
This very moment
Sorrow overwhelms me.
Dancers come now again before me,
Lovely song be heard once more!

Comment
A lament for past glory before Cáo Cāo's tomb. 銅雀台 Tóngquètái, a tower built by Cáo Cāo in 鄴城 Yèchéng, 河北省 Héběishěng. He requested that the courtiers and dancers honor his memory with music and dance before his grave. By the time of the poem the area was derelict. The translation is free adaptation.

Sixty-Two   Hán Yù   韓愈

Zuǒ qiān zhì lán guān shì zhí sūn xiāng
左遷至藍関示姪孫湘   Banished to Lántián

Prayer in admonition
Banished – my reward
It was all for heaven
So there are no regrets.
Snow falls upon me
My home far away.
The horse won't go forward.
If you want to know
Where I ended up
Seek for my bones
In the earth of hate.

Comment

瘴江 zhàng jiāng, river infested with poisoned air, or miasma, i.e. malaria, translated as "earth of hate." 819, Hán was banished to 藍田関 Lántián for a protest he wrote against Buddha, submitted to the emperor. His intention was to protect from harm. The one who wished to love (risking himself by telling the truth) was destroyed.

Sixty-Three   Hán Yù   韓愈

Mǎ yàn gǔ   馬厭穀   The Horse Detests Grain

The palace horse detests grain,
But the poor scholar won't reject husks.
The palace walls wear embroidered glory,
The poor scholar hasn't got a cloak.

They are content in that, and don't think about us.
But if we lose hope, then what happens?
Such a thing must not happen!
Wellaway! Lackaday! cries a fool.

Comment
Written when still a poor student, hoping to pass the examination and better his lot. The point is that the palace horse is overfed with grain, but the poor do not even have husks to live on.

Sixty-Four   Hán Yù   韓愈

Sòng guì zhōu yán dàifū   送桂州嚴大夫
To Yán Going to Guìzhōu

Green woods in 桂林 Guìlín
Far south of the Yangzi
The river like a blue ribbon
The mountains like a comb of green jade.
Doorways adorned with bright feathers
A tangerine tree in each garden
To this far away land of hermits
Could I fly with a Chinese phoenix
A long direct flight?

Comment
Hán Yù celebrates the beauty of the famous region 桂林 Guìlín, Guangxi (in the far south) where his friend has been exiled. Famous for breathtaking views on 漓江 Líjiāng, Li river. In the original, Yangzi is 湘江 Xiāngjiāng, tributary of the Yangzi.

Sixty-Five   Bái Jūyì   白居易   白楽天

Zì yǒng lǎo shēn shì zhū jiā shǔ   自詠老身示諸家属
Happy Old Age

Now I'm seventy-five
We've got fifty thousand coming in
Two of us old now
Family under one roof
Good broth with new rice
Old cotton in the quilted robe
It's an empty old house
But happily we're all together.
I put the blankets by the screen,
The burner by the green curtain,
Listen to my grandchild reciting,
Watch the maid boil the water.
Poems I must reply to –
The brush flies on the paper.
An old robe buys good medicine.
In this quiet way we pay our dues
Scratching the back
Turning to the sun
Nodding.

Comment

846, written in the last year of his life. A poem of contentment in old age, notable for the details of domestic life, with a comment about writing poetry. From the Heian period, Bái Jūyì's poems were widely read in Japan.

Sixty-Six   Liú Yǔxī   劉禹錫

Shítóu Chéng   石頭城   Stone City

The hills stand guard around the old city,
The river-tide beats against deserted wharfs
And quietly withdraws. The Huai flows east –
From long ago, once again, as night deepens,
The moon lifts up light above the balustrade.

Comment
The title refers to an ancient fortified city, now within the city of Nanjing's 清涼 Qīngliáng Park. The river-tide is the Yangzi. 淮 Huái, great river, which actually joins the Yangzi some distance further east. The poem is part of a series.

94

Sixty-Seven　　Liú Yǔxī　劉禹錫

Wūyīxiàng　　烏衣巷　Bird Lane

Near the red phoenix bridge there are wild flowers,
The evening sunlight floods the narrow lane.
In the farmer's courtyards
The swallows come and go,
Long ago they built under princely eaves.

Comment
烏衣巷 a quarter in the south of Nanjing where there were large houses. It had become poorer with the passage of time. The name, literally "crow clothes lane," may have referred to the soldiers wearing dark clothes resembling crows. 朱雀 zhūquè, vermillion bird, Dao spirit-god defending the south, representing summer, here the name of the bridge.

Sixty-Eight   Zhāng Hù   張祜

Rùn zhōu Jīnshānsì   潤州金山寺   Jīnshānsì

A night at Jīnshānsì.
Mist on the water,
Lakes and channels,
The monks return home,
Boat through the moon.
Light of the dawn
On a long white cloud,
Dragon blesses the tower.
The trees on the water,
See them dance.
Heard on both banks
The bell sounds.

Comment
Poet of the late Tang, Zhāng Hù visiting 金山寺 Jīnshānsì temple, located in 鎮江 Zhènjiāng, Jiansu. A beautiful pagoda there, 慈寿塔 Císhòută, which overlooks the lake and waterways. Last two lines omitted, which might be, "If you're feeling sad, at the end of the day, be happy with a glass of good wine!"

Sixty-Nine   Lǐ Hè   李賀

Sū Xiǎoxiǎo mù   蘇小小墓
Before the Tomb of Sū Xiǎoxiǎo

Dew on the orchid like tear-filled eyes,
Was there no one to love you?
No way through that pale shroud,
The lovely flowers unseen.

Here the grass is a carpet,
The pines parasols,
Let the wind be your robe,
Water like jade-beads.

The lacquered palanquin waits for sunset,
The cool green light gleams in vain.
By your grave in 西泠 Xīlíng
The wind brings me rain.

Comment
西泠橋 Xīlíngqiáo, Xīlíng bridge. 煙花 yānhuā, literally "mist on the flowers," could also mean dancing girl. She died aged 19, a great beauty. Someone to have loved her!

Seventy   Dù Mù   杜牧

Tí Xuānzhōu Kāiyuán sì   題宣州開元寺
Visiting Kāiyuán Temple

Long ago the six dynasties flowered here,
But now the plains stretch to heaven.
Unchanging remain the pale sky and drifting clouds.
The songbirds come and go from mountain to stream,
The hills wear their garment of autumn color.
In the gentle water's murmur
Voices sing in sadness and joy.
Autumn once again flings a curtain
Of rain across a thousand roofs.
The sunset strikes the tower –
Sounds a lonely flute.

Comment
開元寺 Kāiyuánsì, temple built in the 6 dynasties (222-589), in 宣城 Xuānchéng, visited by 鑑真 Ganjin Wajo, Buddhist saint (founder of 唐招提寺 Tōshōdaiji, Nara, Japan). I omit the last two lines of this poem.

Seventy-One   Dù Mù   杜牧

Jīnxī yóu   今昔遊   3 Visiting Shuǐxī Temple

水西寺 Shuǐxīsì,
Immortal Li Bai
You wrote about this –
The breeze around the tower stirs
Ancient trees by the cliff.
Three days half-sober half-drunk,
I was letting off steam.
Rain on the hillside unceasing,
Bright the plum blossom
Scarlet red and pure white.

Comment

水西寺 Shuǐxīsì, temple about 50 km SW of 宣城 Xuānchéng, in Anhui. Li Bai wrote a poem about it. 紅白 hóngbái, this may refer to the mingled nature of existence, both weddings (red) and funerals (white), and also the mingled colors of the flowers.

Seventy-Two   Dù Mù   杜牧

Rù Cháshān xià tí shuǐ kǒu cǎo shì juéjù
入茶山下題水口草市絶句   **Below Cháshān**

Along the valley
Over the pass
Under the tall trees.

A small tower,
A sign flag flutters,
The best wine.

Startled mandarins –
A pair take flight,
May they blame me not!

I am left with this
A puzzle in the head
What to do?

Comment
湖州 Húzhōu, town with canals, famous for the tea. 廻頭 huítóu, lit. "circling my head" – two birds above him, or looking back as they go, or the thoughts that arise?

100

Seventy-Three   Dù Mù   杜牧

Chūnrì Cháshān bìng bù yǐnjiǔ 春日茶山病不飲酒因呈賓客
Cháshān Foregoing the Wine

Late spring, enticed by the flute,
I climbed on board the painted boat.
The mountains grand and white clouds in splendor,
The valleys bright with peach in full bloom,
Tea-leaf in bud, and on the point of opening.
Half in shadow, half in sun. But who'd guess?
Here I am, visiting minister, out of sorts –
I'll be a tea-taster on Cháshān.

Comment

Title is literally "Poem for a guest on a spring day, when I was ill and unable to drink at Cháshān." 紅粉 hóngfěn, red and white powder, peach blossom, also the beautiful dancing girls. The topic is really about visiting the pleasure quarters. Dù Mù has a few poems on this theme.

Seventy-Four   Dù Mù   杜牧

Jiāng fù wú xīng dēng lè yóu yuán   將赴吳興登楽遊原
Nothing Better Than Peace

Nothing better than peace –
Gazing at the lonely cloud dispersing,
Quietly chatting with a monk.
So you want to be off?
Seizing the standard?
Before you go, stand on this hill,
And look at the grave over there.

Comment
Two verses praise holiness 清時 qīngshí (pure time), two verses satirize active life. 無能 wúnéng, appears to mean "incapable", but in fact must be "mu" or "wúwéi" capability – equanimity of spirit and detachment. Climb the tower and gaze on the "bright mound," the grave of the second Tang emperor.

Seventy-Five   Dù Mù   杜牧

Chìbì   赤壁   Red Cliffs

The broken pike sunk in the sand,
The blade has not crumbled yet,
You with iron wool and polish,
Find again aflame that time.
If the east wind had not blown
Behind 周瑜 Zhōu Yú so fiercely,
Those lovely sisters 大喬 Dàqiáo & 小喬 Xiǎoqiáo
In that spring season would have fallen
In the hands of 曹操 Cáocāo,
And held in his chamber at 銅雀 Tóngquè.

Comment

This is a thought on the outcome of the battle of Red Cliffs in Hubei (208) – a decisive battle at the end of the Han dynasty. Thank God that Cáocāo (villain) was defeated! The last line is more literally "locked in the tower at Tóngquè." Iron wool is not in the original.

Seventy-Six   Dù Mù   杜牧

Tí Wūjiāng tíng   題烏江亭   Ford at Wūjiāng

There are things not even
The greatest expert
In war can predict.
Bearing the shame of defeat,
Suffering that ignominy,
Fight on, true hero!
East of the Yangzi
Those good lads are waiting,
If you get through, who knows
How it's going to turn out?

Comment
Title refers to 烏江 the ford, in 安徽省 Anhui, where the warlord 項羽 Xiàng Yǔ met his final end, after the battle at 垓下 Gāixià, 202 BCE. Although he had the opportunity to escape, Xiàng Yǔ refused to cross the Yangzi, a fateful decision. In 839, Du Mu is imagining what might have been.

Seventy-Seven   Dù Mù   杜牧

Bó Qínhuái   泊秦淮   A Night on Qínhuái

Chill mist on the water,
Moon cold on the tow-path.
Night on Qínhuái, pleasure quarters nearby.
The girls there know little of that time,
The bitterness of defeat – That old song
"Jade-tree Palace Garden" floats over the water.

Comment

秦淮 Qínhuái, canal in Nanjing. The poem refers to a song 玉樹後庭花 (see poem 28 above) by Chén Shūbǎo, last emperor of the 陳 Chén dynasty (557-589). Nanjing was his capital. He was supplanted by the Sui.

105

Seventy-Eight   Lǐ Shāng Yǐn   李商隱

Dēng lè yóu yuán   登楽遊原   Sunset

1

Evening falls now – a moment only,
So quickly climb the tower to the top.
Boundless in goodness old friend,
Your light brightens all,
Must you go so soon? Stay, go not yet!

2

Day ends and my heart troubled,
Spur to the crest.
The sunset floods the world!
Soon my own day must end.

3

Sunset approaching, quick now
To the hilltop, up the stair;
Miraculous it stands on the water,
The plain lit with gold,
Slowly fading it goes.

106

Comment

Three free adaptations of the same poem on the sunset – as if by one who grieves for his father's death, an older, and a younger poet. 夕陽無限好 xīyáng wúxiàn hǎo, the evening sun lights the world, boundless in goodness; or, how inexpressibly beautiful the sunset is! The hilltop with tower located near 長安 Chángān.

Seventy-Nine   Lǐ Yù   李煜

Yù lóu chūn   玉樓春   Jade Tower Spring

Evening toilet completed this moment
The complexion bright like snow.
Spring banquet and the court ladies
In a line like beads on a string.
Clouds over water cool through the room,
The sound of the panpipes sighing,
Then they play that old song
"Arc-en-ciel robe-de-plume."

Looking on springtime
Who scattered the fragrant petals?
Beating time on the rail, flown by wine,
Let the mood rise till melancholy comes.
On the way home hood the lanterns
Under pure moonlight
Let the horse find the way.

Comment

霓裳羽衣曲 ní cháng yǔ yī qǔ, an old melody, literally "rainbow garments," as worn by the eight immortals, and "feather robes." Tune was said to have been written by 玄宗 Xuán Zōng, (685-762) Tang emperor.

Eighty   Lǐ Yù   李煜

Wū yè tí   烏夜啼   A Nightbird Calls

Heart stone-silent
I climb the west tower alone
Moon like a curved latch.

Thought turns within loneliness.
Tangled in the garden, 梧桐 wútóng.
Autumn, your bright skies now end.

Severed but won't be parted,
Put in order, gone wild again,
Feelings about you on saying goodbye.

What else
Deep in the heart
I can't say.

Comment
梧桐 wútóng, a Chinese parasol tree; Firmiana platanifolia.
李後主 Lǐ Hòuzhǔ, also Lǐ Yù, last emperor of Southern Tang (936-978) imprisoned in seclusion by the 宋 Sòng (960-1279). Grief at the loss of his old life and family.

110

Eighty-One　　Zēng Gǒng　曾鞏

Yú Měirén cǎo　虞美人草　Field of Red Poppies

Behind the jade curtain
Even beauty grows old.
Swords flash as she dances,
Her soul a perfume to heaven
Her blood bright vermillion
Laid a field of red poppies.

Comment
Three lines adapted from poem on the defeat of 項羽 Xiàng Yǔ and death of beauty 虞美人 Yú Měirén. Unwilling to live after his defeat, she performed the sword dance and took her own life – she won't grow old. Her blood turned to poppies. Poignant scene in Peking Opera 霸王別姬 Farewell to My Concubine.

Eighty-Two   Wáng Ānshí   王安石

Zhōng shān jí shì   鍾山即事   Zhōng Shān

Rivulet in the valley run softly,
Slips through the lovely bamboo.
West, the wild flowers gentle
The springtime bring peace!
Under thatched eaves to sit
And wait for day's ending,
How quiet the birds are now!
The mountain still and silent.

Comment

花草 huā cǎo, translated as wild flowers. 鍾山 Zhōng Shān, mountain located to the east of Nanjing, now known as 紫金山 Zǐjīn Shān, Purple Mountain. Wáng Ānshí (1021-1086) lived here in retirement in his last years.

Eighty-Three   Wáng Ānshí   王安石

Chū xià jí shì   初夏即事   Early Summer Impressions

A stone bridge, thatched eaves, a sheltering cliff.
Bubbles break as the stream runs through embankments.
Cloudless skies, a warm breath through the barley.
In the woodland shade bright flowers,
Flowering now even more than in spring!

Comment
即事 jí shì, an impression of things in front of one, a rapid poetic sketch. 湾碕 wān qí, a indented cliff, like an inlet, here translated as sheltering cliff.

Eighty-Four   Wáng Ānshí   王安石

Bó chuán Guāzhōu   泊船瓜洲   Mooring at Guāzhōu

One river between us,
京口 Jīngkǒu and 瓜洲 Guāzhōu.
Only a range of hills to 鍾山 Zhōng Shān.
The spring breeze enlivens the banks,
South 長江 Chángjiāng,
And the moon above,
Will it light my way home?

Comment

京口 Jīngkǒu, ford on the southern bank of the 長江 Chángjiāng (Jingkou district of 鎮江 Zhenjiang city), near the intersection of the grand canal. 瓜洲 Guāzhōu, a ford on the northern opposite bank (near 楊洲 Yángzhōu modern harbor). Chángjiāng, preferred name for the Yangzi or Yangtze river. The place names and river are poetry.

Eighty-Five   Wáng Ānshí   王安石

Hè tí Wūjiāng tíng   和題烏江亭   Wūjiāng Ford

The men are wearied with the long campaign
But this final contest decides all.
Even if our friends east of Yangzi stand true
Will that really win China for the King?

Comment

Another poem on the tragic ending of 項羽 Xiàng Yǔ (232-202 BCE) after defeat at 垓下 Gāixià in 202 BCE. This was a favorite poetic topic. Unlike Du Mu's poem, Wáng Ānshí is skeptical about whether Xiàng Yǔ would have been successful even if he had crossed the Yangzi and escaped.

Eighty-Six   Sū Shì 蘇軾 Sū Dōngpō 蘇東坡

Cì Jīng Gōng yùn   次荊公韻   For Wáng Ānshí

Long way by donkey,
Here we are now on these rough banks.
It was before you fell ill, great teacher –
You said to me, buy land, a small plot.
Good advice then, but it's ten years too late!

Comment
1084. Third verse in a four part series. 荊公 Jīng Gōng refers to a title conferred upon 王安石 Wáng Ānshí. Wáng was advising him to retire from the world and live in peace. Sū Shì visited him, and wrote this 次韻 cì yùn, which is a poem-in-reply with the same rhymes as the earlier poem.

116

Eighty-Seven   Sū Shì   蘇軾   Sū Dōngpō   蘇東坡

Zèng Dōnglín zǒng zhǎnglǎo   贈東林総長老
For the Abbot of Dōnglín Temple

Eloquently voluble the water over pebbles
The stream sings Buddhist prayer,
Gorgeous the autumn,
The mountain his holy body.
Eighty four thousand verses,
Sung last night to light!
But that's a truth which can't be told!

Comment

東林寺 Dōnglínsì, 慧遠 Huì Yuǎn (334-416 founder father of 净土宗 Pure Land Buddhism) established this temple on 廬山 Lúshān in 386. The point being made is that enlightenment is found, not transmitted. This is a verse which had an important influence on later Zen literature.

117

Eighty-Eight　　Sū Shì　蘇軾　Sū Dōngpō　蘇東坡

Tí Xīlín bì　題西林壁　Written on the Wall of Xīlín Temple

To one side the summit,
To the other side the peak,
Near or far, high or low,
The perspective changes.
Will you still not know the true mountain?
Here in the woods lose your way.

Comment

I have taken liberties in interpreting the last line. More accurately, "how can I know the mountain being on the mountain?" The mountain is 廬山 Lúshān. 禅問答 a Zen riddle.

118

Eighty-Nine　　Sū Shì　　蘇軾　　Sū Dōngpō　　蘇東坡

Chìbìfù　　赤壁賦　　Ballad of the Red Cliffs

After a short time the moon rose
Passing between the archer and the goat.
The dew beaded and ran
Upon the river surface
Like flickering moonlight
Heavenly reflection! And our boat
Like a slender reed or pipe
Floated out onward further
As though rising on the wind,
Leaving the world and its worry
Far behind, rising on wings
I felt like an old sage or immortal.

With cups of wine our banquet began,
Happy we struck the gunwales and sang:

A mast of cedar wood
An oar of magnolia
Moonlight on the water
The waves fill with light
They rise up to the stars

Our thoughts hasten forward
The beauty we love
To be looked for in heaven!

There was one with a flute,
Melody phrased to the song:
A voice of regret
A voice yearning
A voice weeping
A voice pleading
Like an unbroken thread
High and long the notes sang!

A grisly old sea-dragon
Hidden in the deep
Would have heard it and danced.

Comment

Excerpt from lines 10-34 少焉月出 to 舞幽壑之潛蛟 from the ode describing a boat trip and a banquet (1082), at the presumed site of the famous Red Cliffs Battle (208), north Yangzi. The battle probably took place near Chibi, Hubei, further south.

120

Ninety   Sū Shì   蘇軾   Sū Dōngpō   蘇東坡

Chū dào Huángzhōu   初到黄州
Arriving in Huángzhōu the First Time

Just to get by I was so busy,
Got to laugh about that!
Coz I'm old now,
And nothing neat and tidy like it was.

The 長江 Chángjiāng flows past these towns,
There's good fish,
Lovely bamboo on the slopes,
And 筍 sǔn just perfect.

In exile what does it matter
If they make me a janitor?
So I write poems as I usually do,
Sitting in the care-taker's office.

Just one thing bothers me,
I'm doing nothing for China –
And I can't understand why they send me
These mouldy old tea-bags!

Comment
Written soon after arrival in exile in 黄州 Huángzhōu, taking up a low-ranking job. 筍 sǔn, bamboo shoot. I have translated "squeezed-out bags of rice-wine lees," as "mouldy old tea-bags." These were given in part-payment and were a benefit.

122

Ninety-One   Sū Shì   蘇軾   Sū Dōngpō   蘇東坡

Dōng pō   東坡   East Hill

Rain has washed the eastern slope,
The moonlight shines clear,
Townsfolk have gone
And only a villager, myself, is here.
Detest not that levée path filled with boulders!
Love rather the sound your stick makes
As the metal end strikes the rocks!

Comment

Written two years after he had moved to Huángzhōu. 東坡 Dōng pō, was the name he gave to the land he was cultivating.

Ninety-Two   Sū Shì   蘇軾   Sū Dōngpō   蘇東坡

Zòng bǐ   縱筆   Not Saying Much Now

Not saying much now that I'm burdened by disease,
My beard white, head bowed under this frosty wind.
My youngest son points. He looks ruddy with health!
But I laugh, it's the medicinal double gin, a red face.

Comment
1099, age 64. In exile on 海南 Hǎinán, he was productive, writing many poems. First poem in a series of three. Original title literally means allowing the brush to move freely on the paper. Title supplied by translator.

124

Ninety-Three   Sū Shì   蘇軾   Sū Dōngpō   蘇東坡

Chūn yè   春夜   Spring Night

So that's it,
Spring night,
A thousand pounds?

Sweet fragrance
& lovely flowers
Under the misty moon.

The band playing
& your voice
So sweet.

Swinging
In the garden,
Deepening night.

Comment

Translated against itself. The original: "A night of beauty, though brief, is worth all." Spring a metaphor for passion. The garden swing a metaphor as well. Let us remember that the girls who worked there often had no choice.

Ninety-Four   Sū Shì   蘇軾   Sū Dōngpō   蘇東坡

Chéng mài yì tōng cháo gé   澄邁驛通潮閣
Looking Towards China

I thought I'd spend my final years in 海南 Hǎinán,
But heaven's king calls my soul to 巫陽 Wūyáng.
Far away on the distant horizon a hawk disappears.
That mountain range, a line painted with the finest brush,
Beloved China!

Comment
澄邁驛 Chéng mài yì, on the north coast, picturing the land in the mind (too far to see). Joy because he has been allowed to return, age 65. 巫陽 Wūyáng is a priestess in the 楚辞·招魂 *Songs of the South*, to whom 屈原 Qū Yuán, the poet (i.e. Sū Shì) must return.

126

Ninety-Five   Lù Yóu   陸游

Xiǎo yuán   小園其一   Garden 1

Smoke from the fields drifts to the village,
A path ascends diagonal through mulberry orchards.
陶 Táo in my hand, reading on my side, still some to go.
A light rain so I'll have to go out and tend the gourds.

Comment

First in a series of four poems, written age 57. 陶 Táo, this is 陶淵明 Táo Yuānmíng (365-427), also known as 陶潛 Táo Qián. 陸游 Lù Yóu (1125-1209) is said to be the leading poet of the Southern 宋 Sòng.

Ninety-Six   Lù Yóu   陸游

Xiǎo yuán   小園其三   Garden 2

Wood pigeons heard
In villages north and south,
The paddies green
With tender shoots.
Ten thousand miles
A long road I've gone,
Here I am now
Taught by the old man next door
How to plant fields in spring.

Comment
Third in a series of four poems.

Ninety-Seven   Lù Yóu   陸游

Shěnyuán   沈園   Shěn Garden

Sunlight lengthens over castle walls
A lonely flute sings.
Here again in this lovely garden
But the old pond and tower have gone.
Under the bridge the green water ripples,
Spring again, my heart sorrows.
It was a picture in the water,
Startled the swan rose and disappeared.

Comment

His love for 唐琬 Tángwǎn is the topic. 40 years have passed. Aged 75 he returns to the garden where he left his famous verse when he met her again by chance, ten years after divorcing her. They had been happily married (aged 20) but were forced apart. She died soon after they met again. He was heartbroken.

Ninety-Eight   Lù Yóu   陸游

Yóu shān xī cūn   遊山西村   Village Festival

Don't sniff,
This old peasant vernaccia,
Cloudy with sediment,
There's no better!
Guests welcome in a good year,
Free-range chicken, best ham.
Hills beyond hills, rivers and streams,
I thought there was no way forward.
Dark willows, bright cherries, here's a village at last.
A spring festival following flute and drum,
The old gentry, young riff-raff, walking together,
A page from how it used to be.
Even now, if the moon would grant me her light,
I'd go back, my stick tapping open the gateway of night.

Comment

Lù Yóu was celebrated for his patriotic poems. At age 42 he lost his position owing to support for military action against the occupation in the north, and retired to 紹興 Shàoxīng, in the country. This is about a village festival. Heart of old peasant China. Perhaps a bawdy reference at the end.

Ninety-Nine   Qián Lóng   乾隆帝

Lú gōu xiǎo yuè   盧溝曉月   Marco Polo Bridge 1

From a thatched roof
The rooster calls up the dawn.
The star river fades
As the dawn light rises.
Three stars of Orion
Descend the sky.
Pale now in autumn
Half-moon stands still.
A mirror cast there – look
Rainbows arch over
Light glimmering water!

Comment
Qián Lóng (1711-99), sixth emperor, Qīng 清 dynasty, reigned for sixty-one years (1735-96), the Qīng golden age. A stone bridge (1192) SW of Beijing, with 11 arches, and some 500 lion-dogs, which look like monks in stoic meditation guarding the bridge. Described by Marco Polo as the most beautiful bridge in the world. First half of the poem.

One Hundred   Qián Lóng   乾隆帝

Lú gōu xiǎo yuè   盧溝曉月   Marco Polo Bridge 2

Monks in contemplation
Crossing the bridge,
Chant spirit in peace.

Lost in home-thoughts,
Travellers start when they see
The moonlight on water.

Going west of the river
They think on the view,
Each time they cross
Still passion at heart.

Comment
心共印 xīn gòng yìn, is freely translated. "Passion" mistranslates 黯爾 àn ěr, worry (the travellers are anxious as they hurry on their way). "Passion" chosen for the nuance in Buddhist and Christian thought. This is the second half of the eight-line poem.

Poets' Brief Bios

A few facts about the poets are offered here. Poems and poets have been chosen somewhat unsystematically, according to the materials that I have had at hand. As I go forward I hope to include translations of all the most interesting poems, and later, to gather them together in one anthology of classical Chinese poetry. I have also included in this list the poets who are found in *Great China 1*.

Chinese history during this period is a vast subject and there is good reference material on the internet. The poets themselves, especially Lǐ Bái and Dù Fǔ (like Shakespeare in English), are at the centre of a great literary universe. Many dates are approximate (?). Japanese name in square brackets. I only give the pinyin names. It is better to follow one system of spelling in English.

Bái Jūyì (772-846) 白居易 also 白楽天 [Haku Rakuten]. A prolific poet who held various official posts, writing critical verse and falling out of favour, being made Governor of Hangzhou, and retiring in old age to Luoyang, close to the Monastery at Xiangshan. Great influence on Japanese poetry.

Cáo Cāo (155-220) 曹操 [Sō Sō] Rose from obscurity to become a military leader, founded 魏 Wèi, one of the three kingdoms, became king. Gifted poet and calligrapher, skilled military strategist and statesman, unifying Northern China. Somewhat merciless, depicted as a notorious villain in Chinese literature and history.

Cáo Pī (187-226) 曹丕 [Sō Hi] Son of Cáo Cāo. First emperor of 魏 Wèi. During his reign the Han empire divided into three kingdoms. Civil administration system reformed under him. Poetically gifted. Fierce rival with his younger brother, Cáo Zhí. Like his father, something of a merciless villain.

Cáo Zhí (192-232) 曹植 [Sō Shoku] Son of Cáo Cāo. Considered amongst the most gifted poets of his generation. Denied a position of influence by his brother, he nevertheless became a leading poet in the 建安 Jiàn'ān poetic school, named for the era (196-220).

Cén Shēn (715-770) 岑参 [Shin Jin] Known for his frontier poems and poetic depictions of landscape. Friend of Du Fu. His son 岑佐公 Cén Zuǒgōng, gathered his poems into 8 volumes 30 years after he died.

Chén Lín (??-217) 陳琳 [Chin Rin] One of the seven scholars in the 建安 Jiàn'ān poetic school. Served as a minister, writing 袁紹 Yuán Shào's declaration of war upon Cáo Cāo. When this was read to Cáo Cāo, it cured him of a headache (and led to his victory).

Chén Shūbǎo (553-604) 陳叔宝 [Chin Shukuhō] Last emperor of the Chén dynasty. Incompetent ruler, preferring wine, women and poetry. Allowed his favorite consort 張麗華 Zhāng Lìhuá, to make important decisions. Defeated by the 隋 Suí, and supplanted by Emperor 文 Wén.

Cuī Hào (704?-754) 崔顥 [Sai Kō]. A friend of Wang Wei and Li Bai. Best known for the verse included here.

Dù Fǔ (712-770) 杜甫 [To Ho]. "The Sage of Poetry." Though from a distinguished family, he did not win an official post until age 43. It was a time of turmoil, and much of his life was spent moving about China. Suffering caused by misrule and hardship was his great theme.

Dù Mù (803-852?) 杜牧 [To Boku]. From a distinguished family, life spent employed in various official capacities, a wide range of writing extant. Delight in the beauty of the world, regret for the past are his themes.

Hàn Wǔdì (157-87 BCE) 漢武帝 [Kan Buti] personal name 劉徹 Liú Chè, [Riu Tetsu]. Emperor Wu of Han, seventh emperor of the Han dynasty. Reigned for 54 years. Adopted Confucianism as state philosophy and ethics. Ruthless in policy. Han China became a powerful and unified nation, of vast territory.

Hán Yù (768-824) 韓愈 [Kan Yu] Mid-Tang poet and man of

letters. Confucianist of strong principle, wrote a letter protesting against Buddhist relics, which led to his banishment south. Celebrated for the informality and wit of his prose style. Promoted ancient classics, friend of contemporary poets.

Lǐ Bái (701-762) 李白 [Ri Haku]. "Poetic immortal." Ranking with Du Fu in fame. Considered himself of Imperial lineage. Individualistic, highly-talented, eventually given a position at court, banished. Romantic and wild in sensibility. His poetry is both amusing and profound.

Lǐ Hè (790-816) 李賀 [Ri Ga] Failed the imperial examination. Friendly with other poets such as Han Yu and Du Mu. Unconventional and imaginative in style, not admitted into the canon of Tang poetry until later. From a short life some 240 poems extant.

Lǐ Shāngyǐn (813-858) 李商隱 [Ri Shōin] Late Tang poet. Worked in the imperial administration. Poetry admired for lyrical sensuality. He wrote a series of poems with no title 無題 which are admired.

Lǐ Yù (937-978) 李煜 [Ri Iku]. Also called Lǐ Hòuzhǔ 李後主. Last emperor of the Southern Tang, taken prisoner in 975 by the Song dynasty. Wrote lyrics of regret for his lost kingdom while held as prisoner. Poisoned by the Song emperor for veiled criticisms in a poem.

Liú Bāng (247?-195 BCE) 劉邦 [Ryū Hō] Also called 高祖

Gāozǔ. First emperor of the Han. Rose from the peasant class as a rebel leader after the fall of the Qin to become emperor. His great rival was Xiang Yu, of aristocratic background, whom he defeated in 202 BCE.

Liú Tíngqí (651-678?) 劉庭琦 [Ryū Teiki] 劉希夷 [Ryū Kii] Passed the exams aged 25. Poet gifted in song and Chinese lute. Said to have been assassinated at age 30 by 宋之問 Sòng Zhīwèn (656?-712?) another poet.

Liú Yǔxī (772-842) 劉禹錫 [Ryu Ushaku] Court official. Poet highly esteemed by Bái Jūyì. Sent into exile, returned to Changan, sent into exile again for satirical poem. Adapted folk songs to poetry.

Liǔ Zōngyuán (773-819) 柳宗元 [Ryū Sōgen]. Employed in a good position, but banished for conspiracy, ending up in Liuzhou, Guangxi. His work was influenced by Buddhism. Celebrated both as poet and essayist.

Lù Yóu (1125-1209) 陸游 [Riku Yū] Court official of the Southern Song, celebrated landscape and patriotic poet. Prolific. The country was controlled by the Jurchen in the north and he wrote on this theme. Plain but lyrical poetry widely admired. Poignant love poetry about 唐婉 Táng Wǎn, his first love.

Mèng Hàorán (689-740) 孟浩然 [Mō Kōnen]. Unlike most of the poets, he did not work in government service but spent most of his life in retirement in his home,

Xiangyang, Hubei. He was well-known to the other poets. Skillful at landscape verse.

Mèng Jiāo (751-814) 孟郊 [Mō Kō]. Passed the examination at a late age. Associated with the poet Hán Yù. Wrote harsh satirical lyrics that are quite different to the two poems in *Great China 1*.

Qián Lóng (1711-99) 乾隆帝 [Ken Ryūtei] Sixth emperor, Qīng 清 dynasty, reigned for sixty-one years (1735-96), Qīng golden age. He was a patron of the arts, establishing extensive collections of art, and also promoted scholarly endeavor and publishing while at the same time imposing a strict censorship. A prolific poet.

Qū Yuán (340?-278? BCE) 屈原 [Kutsu Gen] Statesman and poet in the spring-autumn civil-war period. Known for 楚辭 Chǔcí, *Songs of the South*. These songs are shamanistic spirit journeys. Advocate of alliance with other states, ignored, and spent years in exile compiling poetry. First great Chinese poet. A preface to this book.

Shěn Quánqī (656?-714?) 沈佺期 [Shin Senki] Spent most of his life as a court poet. Often paired together with 宋之問 Sòng Zhīwèn (656-712).

Sū Shì (1036-1101) 蘇軾 also 蘇東坡 [So Tōba]. From a distinguished family of poets. After working for the government as a young man, he was exiled after showing opposition to reform. Despite these difficulties he won a reputation as a leading poet of the Northern Song dynasty.

Sū Xiǎoxiǎo (481?-500?) 蘇小小 [So Shōshō] A courtesan famed for intellect and beauty. She died young. Her tomb was situated at Xilin bridge on West Lake. A romantic heroine in later poetry and drama.

Táo Yuānmíng (365-427) 陶淵明 [Tō Enmei]. From an earlier period, especially admired by the Tang poets. Famous for rejecting the life of officialdom and retiring to the country. Understated and unadorned, his poetry describes an ideal, glimpsed also in his utopian fable, "Peach Blossom Spring" see *Great China 1*.

Wáng Ānshí (1021-1086) 王安石 [Ō Anseki] Song statesman, intellectually gifted. He implemented wide-reaching compassionate reforms on taxation and state provision of education but eventually fell from favor, defeated by bad luck and conservatism. A noble figure, classed as one of the eight great writers.

Wáng Bó (650?-675?) 王勃 [Ō Botsu] From a literary family. Intellectual gifts evident from a young age. Expelled for a provocative submission, died en route to Vietnam, visiting his father in exile. Celebrated for his poems of farewell. His 滕王閣序 *Preface to Prince Teng's Pavilion*, is well-known.

Wáng Chānglíng (698?-755?) 王昌齡 [Ō Shōrei] Well-known

for his frontier poems. Worked as an official in government. Put to death for a satirical verse during the An Lushan Rebellion.

Wáng Hàn (?–726?) 王翰 [Ō Kan]. Worked in an official capacity for chancellor Zhang Yue (663-730). His Liangzhou Songs are minor classics of frontier poetry.

Wáng Wéi (699?-761?) 王維 [Ō I]. Highly gifted at both poetry and painting, passed the examination when still young. Worked as an official, then took semi-retirement at Wang river. Admired for Buddhist spirituality and sensitivity to nature.

Wáng Zhīhuàn (688-742) 王之渙 [Ō Shikan] Well-known for his frontier poems. Acquainted with contemporary poets, Li Bai and Du Fu. Poems popular in his day.

Wūsūn Gōnzhǔ (c. 100 BCE) 烏孫公主 [Uson Kōshu] 劉細君 Liú Xìjūn, granddaughter of Emperor Wudi, married to 烏孫昆莫 Wūsūn Kūnmò, prince of the Wūsūn nomads (BCE c. 105). The Wusun occupied territory in the west, rivals with the Xiongnu, occasional allies with the Han.

Xiàng Yǔ (232-202 BCE) 項羽 [Kō U] Ruthless warlord who rose to great power after the fall of the Qin dynasty. Said to have been of great strength and stature, courageous but foolhardy. Defeated after a long struggle with Liu Bang, who founded the Han dynasty.

Important character in classical drama.

Xiè Língyùn (385-433) 謝靈運 [Sha Reiun] also known as 康樂公 Kānglè gōng, Duke of Kangle. Grandfather was the renowned general 謝玄 Xiè Xuán (343–388). Raised in a Buddhist monastery. Family estate a place of scenic beauty. First great landscape poet. He was known as "Great Xiè."

Xiè Tiǎo (464-499) 謝朓 [Sha Chō] Precocious scholar. Famed as a landscape poet. Highly regarded in his lifetime, "If three days go by and you haven't sung his verses, your breath will stink," said by 梁武帝 Emperor Wǔ of Liáng (464–549). He was known as "Little Xiè."

Xuē Táo (768-831) 薛濤 [Setsu Tō]. A woman poet who became a courtesan after her father's death. Gifted and witty, admired and befriended by the leading poets of the day. She is said to have supported herself by making beautiful paper, used for writing poems.

Yú Měirén (??-202 BCE) 虞美人 [Gu Bijin] The beautiful consort of 項羽 Xiàng Yǔ. At the battle of Gaixia, surrounded by enemy forces, she performed a sword dance, sang a verse and took her own life. Famed in classic drama, featured in TV drama and film.

Zēng Gǒng (1019-1083) 曾鞏 [Sō Kyō] Precociously gifted, said to have written 六論 Liùlùn, "Six arguments," when aged twelve. Worked as an official on historical records, becoming an accomplished historian. Admired for both poetry and prose.

Zhāng Hù (782?-852?) 張祜 [Chō Ko] Late Tang. Little known about this poet.

Zhāng Jì (712-779) 張繼 [Chō Kei]. Passed the examination in 753 and worked as an official. Best known for the poem included in *Great China 1*.

A Brief Note on Tones

For beginners who are unfamiliar with Chinese, here are some brief explanatory comments about Chinese tones (pronunciation) and how they affect these ancient poems. First of all, it should be said that one of the irritations for a foreigner who studies Asian languages, particularly Chinese (or even Korean) is the co-existence of confusingly different romanisation systems. For Chinese, the Pinyin system is now almost universal and this makes life easier. Please follow this. If only the powers that be could see the virtue in having one spelling and using the same characters!

Mandarin Chinese is a language with four tones today. In the past there were more, and the various other Chinese languages have more. Pronunciation does differ with the tone, and so does the meaning. In this book I have followed the accent method for denotation. I give an example.

居	to reside	Jū	Ju1	tone 1	陰平	yīnpíng
菊	chrysanthemum	Jú	Ju2	tone 2	陽平	yángpíng
舉	to raise	Jǔ	Ju3	tone 3	上聲	shǎngshēng
句	verse	Jù	Ju4	tone 4	去聲	qùshēng

One can see immediately that although the sound is similar (apart from the tone) it is the tone that differentiates the meaning, and is all important. The blessing is that nowadays, with computer and internet, the process of study and learning is quicker and easier. The beginner can input pinyin Ju1 (Jū is not accepted in some online systems) to the internet or computer dictionary and various characters come up immediately.

One can listen to different tones, and to readings of the verses, often done very well, at the click of a mouse. There are also readings with characters on YouTube, and some readings of the ancient poems I have translated in these books. The Confucius Centres have excellent readings.

In the past in the West we were told how difficult it is to pronounce Chinese. It is not difficult. Also, it is such a musical language. Listen to the great verses read in Chinese by a good reader with a lovely voice – what delight it is! Though not raised in China, we can speak that music.

The glory of ancient China, the beauty of her language and thought, so long out of the reach of the ordinary person in the West, is within our grasp.

Poem-Title Index

Title	Author	Page
A Night on Qínhuái	Dù Mù	104
A Nightbird Calls	Lǐ Yù	109
A Sparrow and a Hawk	Cáo Zhí	29
After I've Gone	Táo Qián	46
Arriving in Huángzhōu	Sū Shì	120
At Black Tortoise Pond	Cáo Pī	28
At Liángzhōu, Thanking God	Wáng Wéi	61
At a Quiet Place	Xiè Língyùn	49
Autumn Song	Hàn Wǔdì	23
Ballad of the Red Cliffs	Sū Shì	118
Banished to Lantian	Hán Yù	88
Beauties by the Water	Dù Fǔ	82
Before the Tomb of Xiǎoxiǎo	Lǐ Hè	96
Below Cháshān	Dù Mù	99
Bird Lane	Liú Yǔxī	94
Bright for You!	Mèng Hàorán	58
Child Care	Táo Qián	41
Chrysanthemum Wine	Táo Qián	42
Cháshān Foregoing the Wine	Dù Mù	100
Climbing Guànquè Tower	Wáng Zhīhuàn	57
Climbing the Phoenix Tower	Lǐ Bái	69
Courage!	Cáo Pī	27
Double Ninth	Wáng Wéi	63
Dreaming of Lǐ Bái	Dù Fǔ	84
Early Summer Impressions	Wáng Ānshí	112
East Hill	Sū Shì	122
Farewell Wāng Lún	Lǐ Bái	70

Farewell Xuē Huá	Wáng Bó	55
Farewell to Dù Fǔ	Lǐ Bái	79
Farewell to Xīn Jiàn	Wáng Chānglíng	60
Field of Red Poppies	Zēng Gǒng	110
For Lǐ Bái	Dù Fǔ	83
For Wáng Ānshí	Sū Shì	115
For the Abbot of Dōnglín	Sū Shì	116
Ford at Wūjiāng	Dù Mù	103
Garden 1	Lù Yóu	126
Garden 2	Lù Yóu	127
Going Home 1	Táo Qián	35
Going Home 2	Táo Qián	37
Going Home 3	Táo Qián	38
Going Home 4	Táo Qián	40
Happy Old Age	Bái Jūyì	91
House on the Wei River	Wáng Wéi	64
Hunger	Táo Qián	44
In Praise of Wine	Cáo Cāo	26
Jade Tower Spring	Lǐ Yù	107
Jade-tree Palace Garden	Chén Shūbǎo	52
Jewel-stair Complaint	Lǐ Bái	71
Jīnshānsì	Zhāng Hù	95
Jīnzhúlíng Ridge	Wáng Wéi	67
Lament for Lǐ Fūrén (Lady Lǐ)	Hàn Wǔdì	22
Life has No Root	Táo Qián	43
Longing for Home	Wūsūn Gōnzhǔ	24
Looking Towards China	Sū Shì	125
Lǔdōngmén Boating	Lǐ Bái	78
Marco Polo Bridge 1	Qián Lóng	130
Marco Polo Bridge 2	Qián Lóng	131

Mooring at Guāzhōu	Wáng Ānshí	113
Mángshān	Shěn Quánqī	56
Not Saying Much Now	Sū Shì	123
Nothing Better Than Peace	Dù Mù	101
Old Stronghold Yèchéng	Cén Shēn	85
Poem in Seven Paces	Cáo Zhí	30
Poet Five Willows	Táo Qián	33
2 Pure Song of Happiness	Lǐ Bái	74
Red Cliffs	Dù Mù	102
Remembering Li Bai	Dù Fǔ	80
Short verse 2	Dù Fǔ	81
Shěn Garden	Lù Yóu	128
Song for the Young	Lǐ Bái	75
Song for the Young	Wáng Wéi	62
Song of the Battle of Gāixià	Xiàng Yǔ	20
Song of the Flute	Cén Shēn	86
Sorrow at Parting	Qū Yuán	18
Spring Night	Sū Shì	124
Stone City	Liú Yǔxī	93
Storm-winds	Liú Bāng	19
Sunset	Lǐ Shān Yǐn	105
The Horse Detests Grain	Hán Yù	89
The Phoenix Stage	Lǐ Bái	68
Thinking about you	Xiè Tiào	50
To Yan Going to Guizhou	Hán Yù	90
Tower, Yèchéng	Liú Tíngqí	87
Troubled Road	Lǐ Bái	72
Tumble-weed Rolling	Cáo Zhí	31
Téngwáng Tower	Wáng Bó	53
Verse Written at Shíbìjīngshè	Xiè Língyùn	47

Verse for a friend in Changan	Mèng Hàorán	59
Village Festival	Lù Yóu	129
Visiting Kāiyuán Temple	Dù Mù	97
3 Visiting Shuǐxī Temple	Dù Mù	98
Water the Horse	Chén Lín	25
Within Walls	Wáng Wéi	65
Written on the Wall of Xīlín	Sū Shì	117
Wénxìng Hut	Wáng Wéi	66
Wūjiāng Ford	Wáng Ānshí	114
Xiǎoxiǎo Song	Sū Xiǎoxiǎo	51
Yearning 1	Lǐ Bái	76
Yearning 2	Lǐ Bái	77
Zhōng shān	Wáng Ānshí	111

First Line Index

First Line	Author	Page
A night at Jīnshānsì	Zhāng Hù	95
A stone bridge, thatched eaves	Wáng Ānshí	112
After a short time the moon rose	Sū Shì	118
All aboard – cast off, I said	Lǐ Bái	70
All-powerful once	Xiàng Yǔ	20
Alone in a foreign land	Wáng Wéi	63
Along the valley	Dù Mù	99
An autumn breeze	Hàn Wǔdì	23
Autumn again, reliving the time	Dù Fǔ	83
Beam of apricot wood	Wáng Wéi	66
Behind the jade curtain	Zēng Gǒng	110
Behind the western mountains	Wáng Zhīhuàn	57
Boil the beans and prepare	Cáo Zhí	30
Bright towers and silver halls	Liú Tíngqí	87
Chill mist on the water	Dù Mù	104
Climbing the mountain	Xiè Língyùn	49
Close the gate and stay within	Wáng Wéi	65
Clouds in the sky north-west	Cáo Pī	27
Cold rain on the river nightfall	Wáng Chānglíng	60
Death dividing friends is sorrow	Dù Fǔ	84
Dew on the orchid	Lǐ Hè	96
Dismounting and entering	Cén Shēn	85
Don't sniff	Lù Yóu	129
Eloquently voluble the water	Sū Shì	116
Evening and I lower the jade	Xiè Tiào	50
Evening falls now	Lǐ Shān Yǐn	105
Evening sun falls across	Wáng Wéi	64

149

Evening toilet completed	Lǐ Yù	107
Few leave the fort at Liángzhōu	Wáng Wéi	61
Fragrant chrysanthemum	Táo Qián	42
From a thatched roof	Qián Lóng	130
God knows when	Táo Qián	35
Graceful roof, flowering meadows	Chén Shūbǎo	52
Green woods in 桂森 Guilin	Hán Yù	90
Head white with old age	Táo Qián	41
Heart stone-silent	Lǐ Yù	109
Here on this tower	Lǐ Bái	69
How many days have passed	Lǐ Bái	79
Hunger drags me	Táo Qián	44
I thought I'd spend my final years	Sū Shì	125
Illustrious in birth, a line	Qū Yuán	18
I'm in the gorgeous rainbow	Sū Xiǎoxiāo	51
Just to get by I was so busy	Sū Shì	120
Life has no root	Táo Qián	43
Life is short	Cáo Cāo	26
Long ago the six dynasties	Dù Mù	97
Long way by donkey	Sū Shì	115
Longing for you, I'm in Changan	Lǐ Bái	76
Loveliest peony, the dew fragrant	Lǐ Bái	74
Lǐ Bái, who can compare with you	Dù Fǔ	80
Monks in contemplation	Qián Lóng	131
Near the red phoenix bridge	Liú Yǔxī	94
Nobody knew	Táo Qián	33
Not saying much now	Sū Shì	123
Nothing better than peace	Dù Mù	101
Now I'm seventy-five	Bái Jūyì	91
Oak-barrelled tawny	Lǐ Bái	72

On our way then	Táo Qián	37
On the dancing-stage the Phoenix	Lǐ Bái	68
On the quiet sand-bar	Mèng Hàorán	58
One river between us	Wáng Ānshí	113
Prayer in admonition	Hán Yù	88
Rain has washed the eastern slope	Sū Shì	122
Risen on a cloud you	Mèng Hàorán	59
River through hills	Dù Fǔ	81
Rivulet in the valley run softly	Wáng Ānshí	111
Said farewell to you	Wáng Bó	55
Shall I grieve now	Táo Qián	40
Shuǐxīsì	Dù Mù	98
Shàngsì 上巳 performed	Dù Fǔ	82
Silent the silk sleeves	Hàn Wǔdì	22
Smoke from the fields drifts	Lù Yóu	126
So that's it	Sū Shì	124
Storm-winds in tumult	Liú Bāng	19
Sun-up and sunset	Xiè Língyùn	47
Sunlight lengthens	Lù Yóu	128
Tall the lovely bamboo shade	Wáng Wéi	67
Ten days before March	Dù Mù	100
The broken pike sunk in the sand	Dù Mù	102
The heavens in the water mirrored	Lǐ Bái	78
The hills stand guard around	Liú Yǔxī	93
The jewel-jade steps shine	Lǐ Bái	71
The men are wearied	Wáng Ānshí	114
The palace horse detests grain	Hán Yù	89
The sad fife's sweet song	Cén Shēn	86
The tombs of the ancestors stand	Shěn Quánqī	56
There are things not even	Dù Mù	103

There's my front door	Táo Qián	38
To delight in the world outside	Cáo Pī	28
To distant 天 sky I was given	Wūsūn Gōnzhǔ	24
To one side the summit	Sū Shì	117
Tumble-weed rolling	Cáo Zhí	31
Téngwáng Tower, gaze	Wáng Bó	53
Under the Great Wall	Chén Lín	25
Waiting for the day's end	Lǐ Bái	77
When there is life	Táo Qián	46
Winds of sorrow stir the tall trees	Cáo Zhí	29
Wood pigeons heard	Lù Yóu	127
Xīnfēng champagne	Wáng Wéi	62
Young tuxedos to the Jīnshì bars	Lǐ Bái	75

Profile

Stean Anthony

I'm British, based in Japan. I've written a series of books of poetry promoting understanding and peace. Find out more in the MTMM series (*Messages to My Mother 1-7*), *One Hundred Poems, Inorijuzu, Mozzicone 1 & 2, Selections from Shakespeare I–V, Saint Paul 200, Songs 365, Manyōshū 365, Songs for Islam, Gospel 365, Saint John 550, Great China 1, Isaiah Isaiah Bright Voice, Saint Mary 100, Kongzi 136, Saint Mary 365*, Yamaguchi Shoten, Kyoto (2007-12). *Eco-Friendly Japan*, Eihosha, Tokyo (2008). *Monday Songs 1-4, Eitanka 1* (pdf file textbook freely available on website – and sound files). Thanks to Yamaguchi HT, also YH for kind help.

New Projects
Great China 3 (classical Chinese poetry in English)
Saint Matthew 200 (poetic excerpts in Japanese)
Sufisongs (poems for peace in Jerusalem)
Pashsongs (poems by Stean Anthony)
Saint Mary 365 Book 2 (verses for the BVM)
Monday Songs 5 (songs in English for study)

Author's profits from this publication

To be donated to charities working for the enhancement of life quality for all blind and partially-sighted persons in China, including

Hong Kong Society for the Blind
Orbis International
Sightsavers International

My request is that all blind persons be given a free best-quality computer together with advanced training, to increase work opportunities for them, and give ease of communication around the globe.

Books by Stean Anthony with Yamaguchi Shoten

The book is one in a series of translations and adaptations. It is a companion volume to *Great China 1*, also *Kŏngzĭ 136* (poems based on the sayings of Confucius), *Songs 365* (poems based on the Psalms of David), *Songs for Islam* (poems based on verses in the Koran), *Inorijuzu* (Buddhist and Christian words for peace), *One Hundred Poems* (poems based on the Japanese classical anthology 百人一首 *Hyakunin Isshu*), *Manyōshū 365* (translations of ancient Japanese poems), *Saint Paul 200* (poetic phrases from the *Letters of Saint Paul*), *Gospel 365* (based on the Synoptic Gospels), *Saint John 550* (a poetic version of the Gospel of Saint John which can be sung), *Isaiah Isaiah Bright Voice* (sequence of poems inspired by the Book of Isaiah), *Saint Mary 100* (100 poems dedicated to Saint Mary), *Saint Mary 365 Book 1* (calendar of poems on themes relating to Mary, Holy Mother with flower poems, art, prayer, and scripture) and *Selections from Shakespeare,* vols. 1 – 5 (poetic passages selected from the works of Shakespeare). I have also published *Messages to My Mother 1 – 7*, and *Mozzicone 1 & 2*, essays and poems about questions of faith and other things.

MTMM series
GREAT CHINA 2
Poetry from classical China volume two
Translated by Stean Anthony

Company : Yamaguchi Shoten
Address : 72 Tsukuda-cho, Ichijoji
　　　　　Sakyo-ku, Kyoto, 606-8175
　　　　　Japan
Tel. 075-781-6121
Fax. 075-705-2003
URL : http://www.yamaguchi-shoten.co.jp
E-mail : yamakyoto-606@jade.dti.ne.jp

MTMM series
GREAT CHINA 2
Poetry from classical China volume two

定価 本体1000円（税別）

2012年9月25日 初　版

　　　　　　　　訳　者　Stean　Anthony
　　　　　　　　発行者　山　口　冠　弥
　　　　　　　　印刷所　大村印刷株式会社
　　　　　　　　発行所　株式会社　山口書店
〒606-8175京都市左京区一乗寺築田町72
　　TEL：075-781-6121　FAX：075-705-2003
出張所電話
　　東京03-5690-0051　　　中部058-275-4024
　　福岡092-713-8575

ISBN 978-4-8411-0905-4　C1182
©2012 Stean Anthony